Michael Hardcastle

Caught Out

Illustrated by Trevor Parkin

Joel Swift is determined to captain the Shipstone Cricket Club's junior eleven to victory and he wants Carleton Birkby to help him do it. But why is the talented black boy, son of a famous cricketer, such a reluctant batsman? And why does he refuse to bowl?

MICHAEL HARDCASTLE

Caught Out

A Magnet Book

Also by Michael Hardcastle
in Magnet Books

IN THE NET
UNITED!
AWAY FROM HOME
FREE KICK
SOCCER SPECIAL
HALF A TEAM
THE SWITCH HORSE
THE SATURDAY HORSE
ROAR TO VICTORY
FAST FROM THE GATE

First published in Great Britain 1983
by Methuen Children's Books Ltd
Magnet paperback edition published 1985
by Methuen Children's Books Ltd
11 New Fetter Lane, London EC4P 4EE
Text copyright © 1983 by Michael Hardcastle
Illustrations copyright © 1983 by Trevor Parkin
Printed in Great Britain
by Cox & Wyman Ltd, Reading

ISBN 0 416 51930 X

One

Joel Swift took meticulous aim with the rifle and pressed the trigger. Immediately the piano lid slammed down with a tremendous crack and the skeleton at the keyboard began to play a jangly tune. Then Joel turned his attention to a woodpecker on the trunk of a tree. His aim was good again and next instant the bird was loudly knocking its beak into the bark.

'Hey, fantastic, isn't it, Joel!' his friend Edward Tilden yelled with total enthusiasm. 'Look at that old chest covered with cobwebs – down there in the corner on the right. Have a go at that and see what happens! There might be a bomb in it.'

Obediently Joel swung the rifle and pointed it at the miniature bull's-eye target beside the chest and squeezed the trigger. Nothing happened. He must, he sensed, have been fractionally off the target. So he adjusted his aim. This time the lid flew up with satisfying speed and a multi-coloured octopus began to clamber out of the depths of the chest. It was such an unexpected sight that both boys gasped involuntarily and then laughed delightedly.

For his next shot Joel had lined up in his sights a skull wearing a black tin hat and perched on a high shelf. He'd seen someone else fire at that target and so he knew that when a hit was scored the tin hat lifted to reveal a covering of red and green hair, the skull's jaw dropped into a terrible lopsided grin, and, from somewhere behind the shelf, a truly horrible, death-like scream could be heard. But when he pressed the trigger nothing happened. He tried again but the result was the same.

'That's rotten, my money must have run out,' Joel reported sadly, laying the weapon down on the green, baize-covered counter in front of *The Maddest and Merriest Saloon in the Western World*. The proprietor of the stall raised his eyebrows to ask Joel whether he wanted another go. Joel shook his head and turned away with Edward to find some more irresistible novelties in the fairground.

'I still don't understand how those guns work,' remarked Edward as they strolled past a stall offering goldfish as prizes for getting a table-tennis ball into a narrow-necked jar. 'I mean, nothing comes *out* of the muzzle, does it? So – '

'Of course it does, you nut! There's a light in the gun and when you press the trigger it comes on and beams at the target. If you're dead accurate the light activates a photo-electric cell in the middle of the target. And that sets the gadgets working.

Honestly, Ed, I'm glad you're better at cricket than science, otherwise you'd never get into my team.'

Edward wasn't quite sure how to reply to that double-edged compliment so he sensibly said nothing. However, he took comfort from the knowledge that, after Joel himself, he was the best player in the team; he was the only genuine all-rounder because his batting was practically as good as his fast bowling. The previous evening they'd had a training session in preparation for the new season and Edward firmly believed he'd increased his pace. He could hardly wait for the first match to demonstrate that he was bowling faster than ever. Joel, for one, would be delighted.

In his first season as captain of the Shipstone Cricket Club's junior eleven, Joel was determined to win a trophy. The team hadn't been particularly successful in the past but Joel vowed he was going to change that. By recruiting some new players he was, as he put it, 'going to make the competition for places really keen. A player's going to have to be *really* good to get into my team – and stay there.'

For a few minutes the two boys watched the antics of the drivers of the dodgem cars and rejoiced in the more spectacular collisions. Edward suggested that they should have a go but Joel shook his head.

'They cost too much and you can't win anything. I like to get something back for my money. Oh, and my skills.'

'But you couldn't win anything on that rifle shooting,' Edward pointed out. 'And you said yourself that you didn't get much time for your money.'

Joel barely hesitated before replying: 'I was testing my skills, wasn't I? Showing that when I aim at something, I hit it. And I was in total control, Ed. Somebody wasn't going to come up and smash me in the back when I wasn't looking and spoil all my good planning. That's the difference. I was *proving* myself there. So that's what I was getting back for my money.'

Edward decided it wasn't worth arguing with Joel when he was in this mood. In practically everything he did, or attempted, Joel Swift, tall and strongly built in legs and shoulders, was positive and optimistic; he always gave the impression that he wouldn't be defeated by anything.

Edward supposed that's what a successful captain had to be. He didn't doubt that Joel's leadership was just what Shipstone Juniors needed. The previous season the players had simply kept their fingers crossed and hoped for the best in important matches: and most of those important matches they'd lost. Edward was looking forward to enjoying the habit of winning. With his own fast bowling, and Joel's solid batting as an opener, they could have a great season. He wondered if he should suggest that he'd like to be picked as vice-captain. . . .

'Joel, just supposing you had to miss a match,'

he began tentatively. 'Who'd take over as skipper in your absence? I mean, we haven't got an *official* deputy, have we?'

'Don't need one,' was the firm answer. 'I don't intend to miss a single match for any reason in the world. Anyway, I think it would look like favour-itism if I chose a vice-captain. And a captain shouldn't have favourites. We should all be playing for the team, all *equals* together.'

While Edward pondered whether to raise the matter of allowing for possible injuries – after all, even the fittest players sometimes had to drop out after damaging a finger or spraining an ankle – Joel suddenly grabbed him by the arm and stopped dead.

'Hey, just look at that black boy,' he said, his grey eyes, normally so cool, lighting up excitedly. 'That's fantastic! He's hit every one so far – smack on target every time and from all those different angles.'

The boy he'd caught sight of was attempting to win coconuts. He was knocking them off their perches with wooden balls, hurled with venom and accuracy. The most astonishing aspect of his per-formance was that he wasn't throwing from a stand-ing position. All the time he was on the move, darting along the front of the stall and then back again; yet his aim didn't waver. Each ball he shied at the coconuts either struck the fruit itself or the cup that contained it at the top of the pole. Quite a number of people had stopped to watch the action, as mesmerised as Joel was.

'He's not having any luck with knocking 'em to the ground, is he?' observed Edward. 'I mean, from the way he's hitting 'em at least *one* coconut ought to have fallen out by now.'

'That's because most of them will be glued in,' Joel explained. 'It's an old trick at fairgrounds, I

remember my dad telling me. He always said it was a waste of money having a go. So I don't. I expect there's just one loose so that somebody is seen to win now and then.'

'And he's got it!' Edward exclaimed, as a coconut at last toppled from a pole following a direct hit. The scattering of spectators showed their own pleasure in the boy's success by giving him a round of applause. The boy looked surprised and pleased and then clenched his fists above his head in a victory salute. It was only then that Edward noticed what an amazing amount of hair he possessed: it seemed to encircle his head like an ebony halo.

He'd collected his prize from the stall-holder and was walking away when Joel Swift caught up with him.

'Can you throw a cricket ball like that?' he asked without engaging in any preliminary comments. 'I mean, as hard and dead accurate as that?'

'Why do you want to know?' the black boy replied warily. He seemed to be keeping a tight hold of the coconut.

'I'm skipper of Shipstone Juniors' cricket team and I'm looking for good players. I think fielding can win matches – no, I don't just think, I *know* it can. So if you can chuck a ball, a cricket ball, as *devastatingly* as that I reckon you'd be a terrific fielder in the covers.'

The West Indian seemed to hesitate. Then he said, quite softly: 'I don't like batting, man. Tell you the truth, I hate it.'

'Oh well, I don't think that will matter too much,' responded Joel, trying not to show surprise at that unexpected statement. 'We've got me to open the batting and then at No. 4 we've got Jason Lupton. He's not at all bad. Oh, and then there's Barinder. He's really an opening bowler – he partners Edward here – but he's improving pretty fast and he can be reckoned an all-rounder. So we could carry a fielder if he were *really* brilliant. So, do you fancy having a try-out with us?'

Again there was a hesitation before the reply came. 'I might. Where do you play?'

'Our ground's at Wasp Nest Road. That's why we always give the opposition a stinging welcome!'

Joel himself grinned widely at one of his own most familiar jokes but the other boy didn't appear to be amused. Joel was surprised: he'd always believed that West Indians had a great sense of humour.

Edward, who was beginning to feel left out of things, decided he ought to help by asking a few questions of his own now that the conversation appeared to be in danger of breaking down.

'What's your name?'

'Carleton – Carleton Birkby.'

'Do you come from Jamaica?'

Carleton shook his head quite fiercely. 'Dominica, that's where my folks come from. But I was born here in England, just like you, man.'

While Edward paused, because he couldn't think of another worthwhile question, Joel remarked brightly: 'Well, if we get you in the team, Carleton, we'll really have an international side. Barinder's parents came from India and Jamie Gillespie was actually born in Scotland. Jamie's our wicket-keeper, by the way. Not bad at the job, too.'

None of that information appeared to have any effect on Carleton who now glanced pointedly at the glittering gold watch on his wrist and announced: 'Got to go now. Got to get down to the disco.'

'The disco!' they echoed in amazement. Then Joel added: 'You're not a dancer, are you?'

'That's right, man,' Carleton assured them with a wide smile. 'So, I gotta get in shape early. See you around.'

Before he could completely escape them, how-ever, Joel managed to yell to him: 'There's a prac-tice session on Sunday morning at Wasp Nest Road – 11 o'clock. Come and join us if you can and meet the rest of the team.'

As he sped away, the coconut clutched under his arm rather like a rugby ball, Carleton simply gave a kind of half-hearted wave as if to signal that he'd heard.

'Do you think he'll come? Edward asked. 'I mean, he didn't really seem very keen on cricket, did he? What an amazing thing to say, that he *hated* batting. I can never get enough batting. Actually,

Joel, I was wondering about that ... you know, whether I shouldn't perhaps move up the order a bit to get a longer knock. I feel a bit *wasted* at No. 11 and -- '

Joel hadn't really been listening. 'You know,' he said slowly as if Edward had never spoken, 'it's a bit odd, that remark of Carleton's about hating batting because it must mean he's had a go at it. Therefore, he's definitely played cricket. But most cricketers like to chat about *their* game – well, most cricketers *I* know.'

'And me,' Edward agreed. 'Yes, I see what you mean, Joel. He's a bit of a mystery, is Carleton. But perhaps he's just, er, modest and doesn't want to let on that he's really a pretty good cricketer. Some guys are like that.'

Joel was deep in his own thoughts again and he drifted past 'The Haunted House of Horrors' and its grisly advertising hoardings without giving them even a glance. Edward had long ago learned that it was best not to interrupt when Joel was in one of his analytical moods – and an analytical mood Joel was surely in at the moment. Only in his own time would he disclose the result of his ruminations.

Edward would have enjoyed a session on the go-cart circuit but he wasn't going to suggest it, confident though he was he'd be able to out-manoeuvre Joel if they raced against each other round the tight, banked corners. Pace had always been Edward's favourite pursuit, whatever the sport he was engaged in.

'Listen, Ed, I've decided what to do,' Joel announced suddenly in a manner that suggested Edward had been deliberately inattentive to him. 'I'm going to give Carleton a chance as the No. 11 against Empleby in the Knock-Out Cup game. When they're batting he'll get a real chance to show how fast he is around the covers – and from the way he tore away to the disco he must be electric. Our fielding should come on a ton with him in the side.'

'So I'll move up to bat at No. 10 then, Joel?' Edward asked anxiously.

'Well, naturally,' the skipper replied as if such a move had been settled long ago. 'Though against a team like Empleby we're hardly likely to need runs from tail-enders like you, are we?'

Two

When Joel Swift won the toss in the 30-overs-a-side Knock-Out Cup match with Empleby he had no hesitation in choosing to bat. It was a fine day, the pitch looked to be in good shape and, as he pointed out to Edward Tilden on returning to the pavilion, he thought he might as well enjoy a long innings while he had the chance of one. In fact, he was confident he was going to revel in a real run feast for he had a poor opinion of the opposition's bowling resources.

The previous season Empleby had been just about the weakest side in the region. Few of their batsmen ever made a decent score and their attack had been slaughtered on numerous occasions. Accordingly, Shipstone were delighted to have drawn them in the first round of the Cup, especially as that was the competition Joel most wanted to win.

'We might as well get cracking from the start,' the new skipper told his opening partner, Mark

Lockett. 'If we tear into 'em we'll demoralise 'em and probably put up a record total. O.K., Mark?'

Mark, a willowy boy who could produce some elegant shots, particularly off the back foot, nodded his agreement. It was always his policy to endorse whatever his captain ordered; but invariably he then simply followed his own instincts.

Joel finished buckling on his left pad and picked up his favourite bat. His team-mates murmured messages of good luck for his innings, though Joel noticed that Carleton Birkby said nothing at all.

The West Indian boy had turned up at the Sunday morning practice session after their meeting at the fair and proved that he could hit the stumps with a cricket ball as unerringly as he'd shied at the coconuts. His all-round fielding, including catching, was superb and the Shipstone players were vastly impressed. However, Carleton hadn't wanted to bat and so Joel hadn't pressed him. Joel had been rather surprised by the smartness of Carleton's flannels and sweater. But when he'd asked the West Indian if they were new the answer had been a rather aggressive 'No!' So Joel hadn't liked to inquire when he'd worn them previously. To his relief Carleton had consented to play for the team in the Knock-Out Cup match; for even if he didn't bat or bowl he would make a major contribution by saving countless runs with the speed and accuracy of his fielding.

On reaching the wicket Joel tried to exchange a

few pleasantries with the umpires. Although he didn't for a moment expect to influence them into giving decisions in his favour he felt there was nothing lost in showing them that he was friendly and well-intentioned.

The first ball was the traditional loosener and might have been a wide. Joel, however, wasn't going to waste a single chance to demonstrate his mastery – and intentions. He was on to it very quickly and square drove it quite handsomely to the boundary. As the applause from the Shipstone players on the verandah of the pavilion rang round the ground Joel beamed at everyone in sight. He was, he was now doubly sure, on to a good thing with this bowling.

The second ball was of a much better length and Joel contented himself with a comfortable couple of runs. The third ball removed his off-bail with clinical efficiency.

Joel stared at the disturbed stumps with disbelief and dismay. He'd just started to enjoy himself and it seemed to him a tragedy that his innings should have ended so soon. It had looked a perfectly innocuous delivery to him; but, though he wasn't aware of it, the ball had pitched precisely where the bowler intended; it had swung in, just as the bowler dreamed it might one day. So the congratulations being showered on the Empleby player by the rest of the visiting team were thoroughly deserved. The bowler was one of the three new players in the side and already had proved his worth in the eyes of the Empleby skipper.

'Just a fluke, the ball that got me,' Joel remarked unwisely to the incoming batsman, Sean Greene, as they crossed just inside the boundary rope. 'You should be able to cart him all over the place in no time.'

Sean was a thin-faced boy with wide-apart, dark brown eyes. He didn't look like an extravagant stroke-maker – but he was one. He liked to hit the ball; and he could hit it very hard indeed, especially on the legside. As one of his team-mates, a bowler,

had remarked admiringly, 'Sean doesn't hang about when he decides he's ready to start scoring.' Although rather on the small side for his age, he was well-balanced and partial to the sweep and the pull through mid-wicket when launched.

In his eagerness to repeat his feat of the previous ball, the bowler rather over-pitched his fourth delivery. Sean ought to have driven it wide of the close fielders. Instead, he pushed forward tentatively, somehow got a top edge – and then had to stand there, aghast, as the ball steepled before being comfortably collected by the wicketkeeper. The bowler was practically turning cartwheels in his delight at taking wickets in successive deliveries.

Sean trudged away, scarcely able to comprehend how he could have played such an atrocious shot. After all, it wasn't his instinct at all to play so feebly. Why hadn't he struck it away with his usual aggression? He dare not think what Joel Swift would have to say when he reached the pavilion. His only consolation was the thought that the skipper hadn't offered a stroke to the ball that got *him* out. Plainly, this new Empleby pace bowler possessed a very special talent.

The fielding side were still celebrating when Jason Lupton reached the wicket. A left-handed batsman of calm authority, he waited nervelessly as the Empleby skipper, having persuaded his opening bowler to simmer down, altered the field placings. The skipper, who'd made much tactical progress the previous season, had learned the value of treating each batsman as an individual with his own likes and dislikes. He knew that Lupton preferred to play off the back foot and that his favourite shot was the square cut. He signalled gully to move half a metre to his right.

Jason had no intention of being the third victim of a hat-trick. Although he guessed, correctly, that the bowler would over-pitch in his eagerness to claim three wickets in a row, the left-hander was content simply to stun the ball. He recognised that there was plenty of time available for him to pile up a good score. Almost inevitably, the last ball of the over was a poor one: it contained the bowler's disappointment at failing to achieve the first hat-trick of his career. Jason flicked it off his legs and cantered through for an easy single. Mark Lockett, who'd yet to face a ball, frowned as he reached the other end. He'd been looking forward to playing a few shots of his own.

The bowler sharing Empleby's opening attack wasn't much more than a medium-pacer but he dropped on a length immediately. His whippy action immobilised Jason, who'd been expecting some poorer stuff from the second bowler. After all, Jason remembered how feeble Empleby's attack had been the previous season. He'd hit a quick 50 off their bowlers then and he intended to improve on that this time. But, until the last ball of the over, he couldn't force this second newcomer away.

Jason was determined not to allow the bowler the satisfaction of starting with a maiden over. So, although the last ball was also on target, he tried to steer it wide of mid-off; and, instantaneously, he was into his stride, racing down the wicket and yelling 'Come on!' to Mark.

Mark had no intention of moving. He didn't think there was a run in it and, just as important, he was due to face the next ball himself. He was looking forward to that. So he watched, fairly impassively, as Jason skidded to a halt more than halfway down the wicket, glanced anxiously at the fielder and then, desperately, tried to regain his ground. He had no chance. Mid-off, reacting nippily, had snapped up the ball and was arrowing it accurately into the wicketkeeper's gloves. Joyfully, the stumps were smashed down.

'I don't believe it!' Joel gasped in pain and bewilderment. Silence surrounded him in the pavilion for the next few moments because nobody else dared say a word. The scoreboard, however, told Joel the truth: Shipstone, at the end of the second over of their innings, had scored seven runs for the loss of three wickets.

'I'd *never* have run for that! It – it was never on,' remarked Sean Greene. But nobody answered him, either. Sean had already made his own contribution to the disaster.

'Don't try to belt the cover off the ball,' Joel told the outgoing batsman, Tim Elvidge. 'Just play it cool for a bit and stay there with Mark.'

Tim raised his eyebrows at the implied criticism of his style; it really was a bit unfair when he'd done nothing wrong at all so far, unlike some players Tim could mention.

Tim, whose broad nose had once been broken by a cricket ball, was fearless whether batting or fielding as close as the laws permitted at forward short leg. Because of the strength in his fore-arms (cultivated by lots of weight training) he could hit the ball very hard; that, linked to the colour of his hair, had led someone to christen him 'the Blond Bomber'. Tim rather relished the description.

Mark Lockett came across to welcome him to the wicket and offer a few words of advice: 'No good trying to slog the ball yet, Tim. We've got to build a score.'

Once again Tim made no reply. He made his way to the non-striker's end and concluded that Mark, too, was in no position to tell him what to do. Lockett hadn't played a single ball yet.

Empleby's skipper, after conferring for a long time with his successful strike bowler, adjusted the field placings yet again. Confident that his side was on the verge of a great success, he was taking great care to ensure that nothing should go wrong in the planning. His players, he knew, were backing him up to the hilt so he wasn't going to let them down in any way. The few spectators that Empleby had brought with them were applauding constantly and that alone gave the skipper great encouragement. He vividly remembered a Test captain saying, during a television interview, how much the support of the crowd meant to him. Leading his side against Shipstone, he felt exactly the same.

Mark took his responsibility as senior batsman very seriously. Although he conceded that Joel Swift was entitled to be regarded as the No. 1, Mark would have preferred that position to be his own. So, now that Shipstone had crumbled to the calamity of three wickets down before reaching double figures, he sensed it was up to him to repair the damage.

He played every ball with exaggerated caution. Mark was satisfied to display his mastery over the ball; but the bowler was just as happy to have bowled a maiden. At this rate, his figures were going to look marvellous at the end of his permitted six overs.

Tim was fuming. He never had thought much of Mark Lockett's batsmanship – and now he'd just seen Mark waste at least three excellent chances of whacking boundaries. In Tim's opinion, it was criminal to miss any reasonable scoring opportunity, particularly in a limited-overs match. Runs made at the beginning of an innings were just as important as those gathered spectacularly at the end.

The whippy-actioned bowler sent down what was almost a wide with his first ball of the new over, and though Tim swung heartily at it he missed by a considerable margin because he failed to move his feet. Nonetheless, such a poor delivery encouraged his belief that this bowler deserved to be hit. So, next ball, he hit him.

It was a fierce blow. But, as it turned out, not quite fierce enough. Because he hadn't quite got his eye in yet, Tim had made a minor misjudgment. Instead of going for six over mid-wicket, the ball soared to a great height – and then began to drop well inside the boundary rope. As it descended, a fielder arrived at the right spot at just the right moment.

It was Tim's misfortune that the fielder was Empleby's champion catcher, a distinction he'd gained in a pre-season training competition. Now, with his hands properly apart just in front of his chest, he took the ball like a pillar box receiving a postcard: there was no risk of it's popping out again.

Tim, who'd managed to reach the other crease and set off back again while the ball was in the air, groaned loudly. He could anticipate only too well what Joel Swift would be saying at that moment.

Actually, Joel wasn't speaking at all; his head was in his hands and no one in the pavilion felt like saying a word to him about anything. Joel had been certain, as soon as the ball flew upwards from the bat, that Tim was out. The match was turning into a total disaster. His hopes of success that season were falling as fast as Shipstone's wickets.

He opened his eyes to find Barinder Singh standing beside him, a nervous smile replacing his normal happy expression. The Indian boy was a more than competent player of pace bowling and Joel brightened as that thought occurred to him.

'Just stick there, Bari, and don't worry about getting too many runs. Survival is more important than scoring.'

That phrase pleased him so much that he put his arm round Bari's shoulders and accompanied him down the steps. Both of them avoided glancing at the returning Blond Bomber who had succeeded in blowing up only himself on this occasion.

'Best of luck, Bari,' said Joel, sending the No. 6 on his way with a slap on the back. He decided to keep a closer eye on things by strolling round the boundary.

As the batsmen had crossed, it was Mark to face the next ball and he was able to deal with it severely to take Shipstone's total into double figures at last. The sight of his skipper acted as an incentive to do well. He suspected that Joel didn't really like him and would be glad of an excuse to replace him in the side. However, if Mark displayed his best form and emerged from the match as top-scorer . . .

The sun was beginning to spread warmth on what was already a lovely late spring day. Joel, after wandering round almost the entire circuit, perched on a wooden bench on the gentle incline beside the score-box. Things had begun to improve; not by much, but at least they weren't getting any worse. Mark Lockett had started to play a few shots in convincing style and Barinder seemed to have settled in comfortably. Between them, Joel hoped, they might stage a real rescue. They needed to because he didn't have a lot of faith in the remaining batsmen. Jamie Gillespie, the wicketkeeper, was better at making jokes than making runs, except on miraculous occasions; Edward's performances invariably promised more than they provided; and Carleton Birkby had declared that he *hated* batting. Joel hadn't bothered thinking about his own change bowlers because, as he'd told them, they weren't worth thinking about – as batsmen.

He switched his attention back to the match. Empleby's skipper had taken off both his opening bowlers in order to save some of their overs for a final fling if necessary. Joel nodded his approval because he would have done the same in the circumstances. Unusually, the replacements were spinners. Empleby did possess another fast bowler but the captain had decided that an all-spin attack might be a clever tactic at this stage.

So it proved to be. Normally, Barinder enjoyed attacking the spinners. This time, however, he was conscious of the need to keep his wicket intact above all else. Instead of treating a poor delivery on its merits he padded up – and was utterly dismayed to be given out leg before wicket. It happened just as Joel had reckoned that, with the score on 30, a

recovery was in sight. Although Bari had contributed seven useful runs, half of Shipstone's wickets
had now gone down.

Within the span of three overs, three more tum-
bled. Jamie, after clouting one splendid boundary
thought he could repeat the shot at will, danced
down the pitch, missed the ball completely and was
stumped by yards, as his rival wicketkeeper glee-
fully pointed out to him. Joel watched the incident
with horror in his eyes; if he'd had another stumper
he could call on for future matches he would have
dropped Jamie for ever. Andy Ross went without
scoring after swinging at a perfectly straight ball
and missing it; and Steve Brown prodded and prodded until he got an edge and was another victim for
the wicketkeeper.

By the time Edward Tilden was due to go out to
bat the captain was back at the pavilion entrance,
trying to restore morale.

'For goodness' sake, Ed, keep your head down,'
he urged. 'Let Lockie get on with the scoring. Just
don't do anything rash.'

Edward nodded. It wasn't the sort of advice he
relished because he knew he was capable of playing
shots. He wanted to demonstrate that he deserved
the higher place in the order that he'd set his heart
on. But, of course, he had to play for his side.
Perhaps, he reflected as he strode to the wicket, he
just might play a match-saving innings through
putting up an impregnable defence.

He might have accomplished exactly that but for receiving what was undoubtedly the best ball of the entire innings. It pitched just outside the line of the leg stump, kept low, eluded Edward's hopeful push, swung late – and removed his middle stump.

Edward had done well to survive for three and a half overs, he'd even managed to score a couple of runs, but now nine wickets had been lost. And Shipstone's total was only 44.

Dejectedly, Joel watched the team's last man saunter towards the middle. Carleton Birkby didn't give the impression that he would stay there long. Automatically, Joel began to think about Shipstone's bowling strengths. But that didn't bring him much comfort because he knew Empleby's target would be hardly more than a run an over.

As Carleton faced his first ball Joel closed his eyes in expectation of the worst.

Three

It was, naturally enough, an attacking field that greeted Shipstone's tail-ender. Players clustered as close to the bat as they were allowed and the Empleby skipper edged ever nearer as his bowler trotted in for what they fondly hoped would be the last ball of the innings.

Carleton, his bat firmly pressed against the turf, appeared quite unconcerned until the ball pitched short and wide of the off-stump – whereupon he stepped out and drove it all along the ground to the mid-off boundary. It was a handsome as well as a fiercely struck shot. The batsman, however, gave no sign that he was pleased with it as he resumed his stance.

The Empleby captain could only suppose that the stroke had been in the nature of a fluke: No. 11's didn't play shots like that by design for otherwise they wouldn't *be* No. 11's. That was unarguable logic to him. So he said nothing to his bowler as the off-spinner trundled in and this time pitched the ball up a bit further. Once again Carleton moved nimbly into position and, with a lovely, wristy action, square-cut the ball firmly for a second successive four.

This time the fielders weren't the only ones to blink. In the pavilion, where he'd been on the point of telling his wicketkeeper about some changes he had in mind, Joel wished there could be an 'action replay' on a television screen of the way the West Indian had played those two shots. It was hard to believe they'd been as good as he thought they were! And those boundaries had come from a boy who claimed to hate batting!

Against all expectations, the Shipstone total had now passed 50 and Joel leapt out on to the verandah to make a point of leading the applause. He wanted Carleton to know that his effort was appreciated. He regretted not wishing him luck earlier.

'Hey, do you know something?' Jamie inquired generally. 'Carleton's now our second top-scorer! Not bad for a No. 11.'

Mark had so far not said a word to his new partner. After all, he hadn't expected him to last out the over, let alone hit a couple of boundaries. Now he wondered whether Carleton might just manage to survive long enough to enable Mark himself to make a decent score. Before the start of the next over he strolled down the wicket for a word with him.

'You can leave the scoring to me now,' he

announced pompously. 'There's no need for you to take any risks. Just keep your end up. O.K.?'

There was the merest hint of a grin around Carleton's lips as he replied, 'I won't be taking any risks with this bowling, man.'

Nor did he. During the course of the next half-dozen overs he patiently waited for the hittable ball – and hit it with strength and timing that couldn't be faulted. Invariably he placed it so well that fielders always had to turn and chase. Rarely did the ball fly above knee-height because Carleton's style was to keep it on the ground whenever possible. At first reluctantly and then with resignation, the fielders dropped back until Carleton could have taken singles to almost any point at will. Empleby were now more concerned with stemming the flow of boundaries.

Their skipper bit his lip, hard, as he worried about how to deal with the problem. He hadn't thought it necessary to bring back his opening attack but now he hardly had a choice. If, however, this last pair survived the remaining overs from his opening bowlers Empleby might be in deep trouble. It was an indication of how well the batsmen were going that he could suppose that they *might* hold out against his very best attacking bowlers. Still, in the circumstances, he just had to risk that – and hope for the best.

'Can't see why he said he *hated* batting,' Edward remarked as Carleton suddenly cut loose by pulling

33

a ball for six over square leg. 'Anybody who can do that *must* be enjoying himself!'

'Anybody who can hit like that *must* have batted before – and higher up than last man,' said Tim Elvidge, a trifle sourly as he remembered his own bad luck in the way he was dismissed.

Joel was thinking along similar lines. Carleton was displaying the strokes and the technique of an experienced batsman: he certainly wasn't gathering his runs from lucky swings and snicks. But why, when he could play so well as this, did he resent batting at all? Joel sighed. He could think of no answer. What he did know was that if only Carleton Birkby had gone in much earlier – say at No. 3 or 4 – then Shipstone would have had a huge total on the scoreboard by now. As it was, every run was still vital if they were to have a chance of winning the match.

Even with the return of the main strike bowlers, the scoring rate didn't slow down. To Carleton, sheer pace seemed no harder to cope with than off-spin. Mark was in no difficulty with it, either, so the tenth wicket pair continued to prosper.

The end was unexpected. The partnership reached 50 when Carleton drove the ball back past the bowler and they took two fairly unhurried runs: and, in doing so, Carleton's own score went up to 35, one ahead of Mark's total. Naturally, the applause from the Shipstone players and supporters was prolonged. After losing nine wickets for only

44, the side was now in sight of reaching 100, a target that had appeared impossible half-an-hour earlier. The next ball was the first of a new over and Mark flicked it away behind his legs. Then, after advancing a couple of paces down the wicket, he halted.

It was Carleton's call and he could see that there was an easy run to be had because the wicketkeeper was the only fielder within reach – and he had some distance to move. Yelling to his partner to run, Carleton sprinted down the pitch. But Mark was motionless, his head turned towards the stumper. By now the ball was in the keeper's hand and so Mark hurriedly retreated to regain his crease.

Carleton, seeing that he wasn't going to get any support from Mark, managed to stop and, in the same movement, turned and dashed back towards safety. Because of his speed he would have reached it, too, if the stumper hadn't thrown the ball so accurately to the bowler guarding the wicket at the non-striker's end. The West Indian dived headlong but, even as he launched himself, the bowler triumphantly shattered the stumps to the accompaniment of the loudest 'Howzat?!' of his career to date.

The umpire didn't hesitate before his finger went up.

Shipstone, 94 all out, last man 35.

'Sorry, Carleton, I just didn't think there was a run in it,' Mark apologised as they walked in together. 'I can't run as fast as you, you see.'

'Why didn't you tell us you could bat as well as that?' asked Joel, slapping his top-scorer on the back.

Carleton had another of those half-smiles on his lips that were becoming his trade-mark. 'Didn't know that myself, man,' he replied enigmatically.

Joel for one didn't quite believe him but he wasn't going to say so. 'Well, you've given us something to bowl at, that's for sure. Empleby have got to aim at more than three runs an over and I reckon we should be able to keep 'em under that – just so long as we bowl and field at the top of our form.'

Those words were intended to stimulate his team-mates. They, however, needed no extra encouragement; they were as keen to win the match as he was. Edward Tilden, in particular, wanted to demonstrate that, having failed with the bat, he was going to succeed with the ball. His pace, he was certain, would be greater than anything generated by the Empleby bowlers.

Joel tossed him the ball and then deliberated with him for several moments on the matter of field placings. In fact, these had been worked out in detail before the match even started but Joel liked, as he put it, 'to keep their opening batters on tenterhooks as long as possible'. He had decided that Carleton should patrol the covers but he made a point of telling the Shipstone batting hero to drop back until the bowler ran in – and then Carleton should advance as stealthily as possible.

'Whatever you want, skipper,' was the rather unexpected response.

Edward was quite pleased with his first ball. Although it could be regarded as a loosener, he got his line right; the batsman blocked it carefully, almost suspiciously. The next two deliveries were also treated with exceptional respect and Edward's spirits, already high, rose still further. After all, he wasn't expecting to reach maximum speed until the middle of the following over. He knew that it always took time for a top bowler to find his rhythm and then reveal his most devastating pace.

Empleby's perfectly sensible plan was for their openers to play themselves in before thinking about scoring rates. It was essential, their skipper argued, not to lose early wickets (after all, he'd seen what early disasters had done for the Shipstone innings; and, in his opinion, they'd been very lucky not to be all out for under 50). He had an idea that Shipstone bowling would deteriorate if they didn't manage a breakthrough fairly quickly.

So he wasn't at all pleased when his batsman flashed unwisely at the last ball of the over. It could safely have been left alone. Instead, he got a touch and the ball flew to the right of the wicketkeeper. Jamie Gillespie took off in spectacular goalkeeping fashion but wasn't able to grasp the ball. As it bounced off Jamie's over-large gloves the batsman, who hadn't dared move, wiped imaginary sweat from his brow with the back of his hand.

'I'd've snapped that up if you hadn't got in the way,' said Joel, through clenched teeth, at first slip. He might have done, too, because he didn't drop much.

'The guy'll get over-confident and think he can get away with anything,' Jamie retaliated, not at all abashed by his error of judgment. 'We'll have him out in no time, you see.'

'You'd better be right,' was Joel's grim comment as they strolled to the other end of the wicket. Both commiserated with the unlucky bowler.

Edward had an awful feeling that it wasn't going

to be one of his days. He didn't like to admit it but he was much affected by such matters as whether his luck was in or out. In the present situation he knew he was definitely unlucky that it was the last ball of the over; now he wouldn't have an immediate chance of cashing in on the batsman's unsettled state.

To his team-mates, Barinder was often known as 'Smiler' but, after his first over, he was only half-pleased with the way the world was treating him. No runs had been scored off him but he hadn't taken a wicket. There'd been a couple of scoring chances but the batsmen had declined them. Bari, of course, couldn't complain about that.

With those orders from their skipper to dig in weighing ever more heavily on their shoulders, the batsmen gradually sank deeper and deeper into a sort of trance. They concerned themselves only with protecting their stumps. They offered hardly an aggressive stroke between them in the course of the next six overs. The runs that came their way were the result of chancy prods and pokes and an even flukier inside edge that missed leg stump by the width of a pencil point.

Joel was in a dilemma. The Empleby team were pinned down, they were struggling like fish in a net and getting nowhere. Normally, he would change his bowlers at this stage of a limited-overs match because they had only two left apiece.

'What do you think, should I give you another over now to keep the pressure on?' he asked Edward in a low voice. 'Or do you want to come back fresh later?'

'Oh, I'll keep bowling,' was the eager reply. 'I'll put everything I've got into this over. Oh, and Joel, do you think we ought to move Carleton a bit closer – to short extra cover, perhaps, or even silly mid-off – to put the squeeze on a bit more?'

'Good idea, Ed. They'll have to start hitting out soon and Carleton's the guy to cut off the runs.'

The move worked like a charm. Edward, delighted by Joel's ready acceptance of his suggestion, produced a good ball that the batsman was thankful to be able to push away to the off-side. Carleton turned to retrieve it and apparently stumbled. It seemed as if the ball was past him – and there might even be a run in it for a batsman desperate to start scoring. He teetered forward a couple of paces, eager for a response from his partner.

In that instant while the batsman was out of his ground Carleton swooped. In one fluid movement he seized the ball from some point behind his right ankle, twisted, aimed and wrecked the stumps with the force of his throw.

The batsman simply gaped as the umpire, deeply impressed by the scintillating style of the fielder, raised his finger and, for good measure, intoned: 'Out – quite definitely out!'

Although he couldn't claim the wicket in his final

analysis, Edward was as overjoyed as every other member of the Shipstone team. With, that is, the exception of Carleton himself. He just shrugged his shoulders as if he didn't understand what all the fuss was about when the deluge of congratulations cascaded over him.

For Empleby, the loss of that first wicket was soon to prove an unexpectedly severe blow. Having been warned by his captain not to take any chances in hitting the ball away to the off, the next batsman deliberately tried to steer everything towards the on-side. Thus, in attempting to fend away a decent ball that lifted a bit, he foolishly steered it straight into the eager clutches of Tim Elvidge at forward

short leg. The corn-haired fielder flung the ball almost as high as a steeple in his joy at taking the simple catch.

In the course of the next three overs two more batsmen departed in unheroic circumstances. With Empleby beginning to fall behind the clock, both felt they should force the pace and get their team back into the game. A harmless delivery from Bari, now tiring after a longer opening spell than usual, was struck wildly straight back at the bowler; and, to his own amazement and relief, Barinder hung on to it in the pit of his stomach. Then, with only two runs added, the next victim also took a great heave at the ball, missed it completely and turned to find his leg stump horizontal.

If Empleby were to have any chance at all now of winning the match everything really depended on their skipper. He had played himself in cautiously and was looking for runs. However, Shipstone's medium-pacers, Andy Ross and Steve Brown, were carrying on the good work of the openers and pinning the batsmen down. Andy, as Joel was to tell him later, had rarely bowled better. And it was he who produced the ball that got rid of Empleby's remaining danger man. When the batsman aimed to flick the ball away square of the wicket it turned more than he'd expected; he wasn't fast enough to change his stroke, the ball flew off the shoulder of the bat and Joel Swift took a neat catch just above head-height at slip.

After that, there wasn't a great deal of resistance left in Empleby. Their innings subsided rather than collapsed as each of the remaining batsmen dabbed away to score a run or two and even, in a couple of cases, a boundary. Joel and his bowlers were able to maintain the pressure and the outcome was inevitable. When the end came, Shipstone had triumphed by the surprisingly wide margin of 51 runs.

'We'll probably have to play a lot better than this to win our next Cup match,' Joel commented to Edward when they and the rest of the Shipstone players had finished congratulating each other on their overall success. 'But for Carleton's batting – oh, and that fantastic run-out that broke their opening partnership – we really could have lost this game. Terrible thought, that.'

'Are you planning to move him up the batting order for the next game, then?' inquired Edward, trying his best to keep any trace of envy out of his voice.

'Well, I think I ought to but I honestly don't know whether he'd agree to it. I don't know whether he still hates batting after that performance today.'

Joel paused, reflectively. Then he added in a firm tone: 'There's still an awful lot we don't know about Carleton Birkby. He really is a mystery. But, Ed, it's a mystery I intend to solve as soon as possible.'

Four

With the utmost care and the straightest possible bat, Edward Tilden played down the line of the delivery. Yes, he assured himself, that felt fine. He was positive he was playing correctly. So now he repeated the stroke in slow motion – and this time he watched his own image in the mirror. Again, all appeared well. Surely there wasn't a hint of daylight between bat and pad. Therefore, that defensive shot was perfect. Well, as perfect as anybody who wasn't opening the batting for England could make it.

The full-length mirror was fixed to the wall of the entrance hall in Edward's home. It was there, really, for his mother's benefit because she was a model and unfailingly checked her appearance every time she left the house. To Edward, however, it was just as useful because, with its aid, he intended to improve his batting technique. Recently he'd heard on a local radio sports programme a leading batsman relate the story of how he'd cured a serious fault in his armoury of strokes by practising in front of a mirror. He had spotted the flaw in his backswing which was causing him to play *across* the line of the ball.

Edward was determined to eliminate every weakness in his own batting so that he could move up the order for Shipstone. After Carleton's great success in the Cup victory over Empleby the previous week it was obvious that the West Indian boy wouldn't be dropped to the No. 11 spot again. So Edward had to be sure he wasn't a candidate for the vacancy.

Although he and Joel Swift had been close friends for a couple of years he was well aware that Joel was not influenced by friendship alone when selecting the batting order. Edward could only hope to improve his position by merit. He'd been unlucky to get such an unplayable delivery in the Cup match and he thought Joel ought to take that into account when picking the next team. But Edward doubted that he would. His main intention, therefore, in the next few League matches was to score some runs *and* not to lose his wicket under any circumstances. The skipper must see for himself that his opening bowler was *greatly improved* as a batter.

Because he'd been thinking about Joel so intently Edward was quite startled to hear his voice only moments later. As it was such a lovely warm day the front door had been left open. Now, after an arrival as silent as a ghost's, Joel was standing in the porch watching his team-mate go through the motions of playing a perfect straight drive.

'Er, what did you say, Joel?' Edward asked when he'd recovered most of his composure. If someone was going to catch sight of him engaging in a secret practice session in front of a mirror, he'd have preferred it to be anyone but the captain of his own team.

'I said I was glad to see you having an indoor net,' replied Joel with the widest of his grins. 'After the way you got yourself out against Empleby you need all the batting practice you can get!'

'Oh, come on, Joel, that's not fair! The ball that got me out was the best one bowled in the entire match! I mean – '

'We *all* say that, Ed, even if it was actually a stinker,' was the mild reply. 'Anyway, doesn't matter how good it was. So don't take it so seriously. I play you for your bowling, not your so-called batting.'

Edward couldn't help feeling thoroughly despondent. He knew that Joel would be sure to remind him about the mirror-practice next time his wicket fell. The way things were going, he hadn't a hope of getting a lift up the batting order unless a miracle occurred. And his mother, for one, was forever insisting that miracles *never* happened to those who needed them most.

'Listen,' Joel was saying eagerly, 'we've got a

great chance to discover more about Carleton Birkby. You remember I told you I was going to investigate? Well, I found out that he's entered for a disco dancing contest at Ashfield Park this afternoon. It's on at the open air theatre as part of the Bank Holiday entertainments programme. In fact, it starts in less than an hour. That's why I came round to see you, Ed. Thought you might like to come along and see what happens. Between us we could learn a lot about Carleton – the sort of stuff he'd never tell us himself, judging by the way he's so, so *secretive* about everything. O.K.?'

'Oh, yes, great!' Edward responded, brightening considerably. It was good to know that Joel thought of him as a companion before anyone else. So, for the moment, perhaps he ought to suppress his batting ambitions and help the team in another way. At the same time, he himself was quite keen to fathom the mystery of Carleton's background. 'I'll just put my gear away and then we can go to the Park immediately if you like. I hadn't anything else planned for this afternoon.'

'That's what I expected,' Joel said in a level tone.

Although Ashfield Park was just beyond the town centre and quite some distance from where Edward lived, Joel had decided that they should walk all the way. When you're walking, he pointed out, you could think and talk; when you went by bike you had to concentrate on the road all the time because of crazy motorists who had no compunction about clobbering cyclists. Edward didn't mind the walk; it provided an ideal opportunity to discuss the team and its composition with the captain and sole selector.

'What do you think we should do about Sean Greene?' Joel asked in a deceptively casual manner as they came out of a corner shop where he'd generously treated Edward to a bar of chocolate because he'd bought one for himself. 'Out first ball when he should have been digging himself in, especially after we'd just lost my wicket. He really does need to be restrained, does Sean. It was the start of a slide, you see, when he was out.'

Edward nodded and tried to come up with a rapid solution to the problem. It didn't take him very long.

'Well, we could move him down the order, Joel. Then, you see, someone else could move up and . . .'

'No, that's no good,' Joel cut in. 'That's poor thinking, Ed. Sean would hit out all the quicker just to prove he could do it. And, down there, he'd have less time to score his runs. No, the *sensible* move would be to promote Sean to open the batting with me. That would instil a sense of – of responsibility into him. Make him realise that he needs to look at the bowling, to sum it up, before he starts belting it.'

Edward couldn't deny the sense in that suggestion. He just wished he'd thought of it first instead of his own offering. He ought to have remembered that Joel was a believer in positive, not negative, policies.

'How did you discover that Carleton is competing in a disco contest?' he asked in order to change the subject. 'I mean, it's not something you're keen on, is it?'

'A girl at my school is a fanatic about disco dancing. I overheard her talking about the contest and saying that the one they'd all have to beat was a West Indian boy called Carleton Birkby. So I got the details from her. She says she's seen him in action a few times and he really is terrific. So good he ought to be on television.'

When they reached the Park it seemed that the whole town had arrived ahead of them. Because he'd been thinking about cricket and very little else, Edward hadn't imagined that so much would be going on. There was a miniature fairground, a hockey tournament, a tennis tournament and a comedy wrestling show. The greatest attraction, however, was undoubtedly the disco contest in the open-air theatre. Practically every vantage point on the steeply sloped grassy bank opposite the stage had already been taken by excited teenagers; others appeared to be encircling the stage itself in one vast embrace. As the music blared out the clutching ranks began to sway rhythmically; and the tempo increased dramatically with the chanting encouragement of the masses on the hillside.

'Hope this doesn't go on too long or I'll be deafened before it's over,' Joel remarked, as he shouldered his way into the audience. Edward looked blank so Joel supposed he hadn't heard. Well, that was to be expected in the circumstances.

When the contestants began, one by one, to perform, Joel had no idea exactly how they were being judged. Some of the more spectacular dancers seemed to be in conflict with the accompanying music rather than in accord with it. A few tried to do too much and paid the penalty with crashing falls or burning slides across the arena. Those who produced the highest leaps or the fastest somersaults earned the loudest cheers. But maybe, Joel thought, those weren't the feats that gained the highest marks.

'What do you think of it?' Edward managed to ask.

'Not much,' was Joel's shouted reply. 'It's not as thrilling as cricket!'

A girl with glitter on her face who was standing beside them looked totally amazed at that comment. Then she turned to her friend and hissed, 'Craziest guys I ever heard.'

Then, to what sounded like an additional chorus of cheers and screeches, Carleton Birkby emerged down the short avenue of flickering, multi-coloured lights to reach the centre of the stage. As with every other competitor, the announcer gave him a brilliant build-up. The difference this time was that the West Indian boy with the mushroom hairstyle deserved it.

Although he occasionally put in a high (and sometimes sideways) leap for effect, Carleton seemed to flow across the stage where others had jinked and raced; yet all his movements were astonishingly fast. To Joel, not the least surprising thing about the act was Carleton's choice of attire; white shorts, white knee-socks and a white T-shirt, with red-and-green diagonal lines, like a sash. There was no paint on his face or forehead, no jewellery or sparkle on hands or knees; and that, too, made him different from most of his rivals.

Then, just when it seemed that his act was coming to the end, he produced a totally original gimmick: a cricket ball! Nonchalantly, Carleton tossed the shining red ball high in the air, spun round twice and then caught it one-handed as it came down. He repeated the trick with the other hand and then added a variation by taking the ball even as he was squatting almost on his haunches.

'Terrific!' yelled Joel, joining as enthusiastically as anyone in the renewed applause.

'That's why he must be wearing a white outfit, because of the cricket,' Edward shouted in reply. 'Great idea. He's got to win, Joel!'

Joel nodded his agreement. It hadn't occurred to him that the white shorts and socks were the equivalent of a cricket motif but he could see it now.

Carleton rounded off his performance by hurling the ball to its highest point yet; and then darting from side to side before grabbing it just as it was about to hit the stage. Not once had there been a semblance of a mistake in his rhythmic 'fielding' and that, combined with his flair and style, made him the obvious favourite for the first prize.

In common with many other spectators, Joel and Edward watched the remaining contestants with minimal interest. They were simply waiting for the announcement of the results.

The roar of approval that greeted the news that Carleton had been awarded first place was thunderous. 'Nobody else really stood a chance,' Joel yelled at Edward. They continued to applaud as Carleton was summoned to the centre of the stage to be presented with his prizes: a statuette and vouchers to be exchanged at a local store for records and clothing.

'Come on, Ed, let's go and congratulate him – show him his team came to support him,' Joel insisted, starting to push his way out of the crowd which was waiting for the next contest in another age-group to begin.

They made their way round to the back of the theatre where parents and other relatives and friends were gathering to greet the performers as they emerged from the dressing-rooms. A tall black man was leaning in a casual way against the outer wall and signing a piece of paper for a fair-haired

small boy. To Edward, there was something faintly familiar about the man. He looked round and saw another adult watching the scene with obvious great interest.

'Excuse me,' he said, going over to the spectator, 'but do you know who that man is?'

'You interested in cricket, boy?' was the immediate response.

'Of course.'

'Then, man, you should *know* who that is. That's Ralph Robertson Birkby, one of the greatest cricketers of all time. Should have played for the West Indies a hundred times but, oh man, was he unlucky! He sure was. But you'll never see a better batsman as long as you live, man.'

Five

Joel's eyebrows shot up when he heard that claim made with so much pride but before he could join in the conversation Carleton came lightly down the steps from the stage door, holding his statuette happily against his chest. There was a burst of applause from some of the waiting families and Carleton responded with a grin and a high lift of his shoulders.

In an instant, Ralph Robertson Birkby was at the foot of the steps to greet the boy with a hug as enveloping as a bear's. He actually lifted Carleton off his feet.

'Great effort, son, great effort! I just knew you'd be the winner soon as I saw the way you were conducting yourself.'

Then, over his father's shoulder, Carleton caught sight of Joel Swift watching him. For a moment, their eyes locked. There was a second or so when Joel suspected that Carleton wasn't going to acknowledge him. But, suddenly, the West Indian boy produced a huge wink.

'Congratulations, Carleton,' Joel said, going forward as Mr Birkby at last released his son. 'That was really terrific.'

'Terrific,' Edward echoed. 'Best dancing I've ever seen in my life – and your catching. Well, out of this world.'

Ralph Birkby had turned to see who was lavishing praise on his son. When he shook hands with them it was with the firmest of grips.

'Better tell me who I'm meeting, Carleton,' he said pointedly.

The introduction by Carleton was rather mumbled and consisted of simply their first names; but Mr Birkby didn't seem to mind.

'You look like cricketers to me,' he said confidently. 'That right?'

'Definitely,' replied Joel, pleased with that immediate identification. 'In fact, mine – er, ours – is the team Carleton played for last week in the Cup match.'

'Guessed as much. He admitted he'd helped out in a team that was short of players.'

Joel recovered rapidly from his initial surprise at that remark and started to explain: 'Oh, it was more than that, Mr Birkby. I mean, he's a *brilliant* – absolutely brilliant – fielder. And then his –'

'Carleton, what was your prize for winning the contest?' Edward interjected loudly. He had noted something Joel must have missed in his eagerness to talk to Mr Birkby: the desperately anxious expression on Carleton's face. It was perfectly plain to Edward that, for some mysterious reason, Carleton didn't want his father to know the details of the part he'd played in the defeat of Empleby.

'Oh, money for a new outfit – and some new music,' Carleton said with a look of gratitude at Edward. 'Hey, Dad, I sure am thirsty. Think we can go and get a long, long drink at the refreshment place over there?'

'Right, man, you've earned it,' said his father, putting an arm round his shoulders. 'Your buddies here can come and have one too, on me.'

Edward, ignoring a puzzled look from Joel, was wondering how he could broach the subject of Mr Birkby's career as a cricketer. He'd heard of most of the great West Indian batsmen such as Sir Gary Sobers and Viv Richards and Clive Lloyd. But never had he heard a word about a player called Ralph Robertson Birkby.

When Mr Birkby had bought their drinks, and what he described as a 'double-strength Coke' for himself, they sprawled on the grass bank beside the open-air café. Joel wasted no time at all in asking Mr Birkby whether he still played cricket.

'Oh sure, when I get the chance, Joel. Reckon I'll go on playing cricket till I die 'cos it's in my blood – and my bones! But I'm in the shipping business, see, and that means I have to travel a lot, often to places where they don't fancy cricket at all. Crazy,

I know, but that's the way it is in places like Sweden and Belgium and Switzerland. Denmark now, they've got a bit of sense – got one or two quite good players. But not enough of 'em, worse luck. So, no, I don't get to play half as much as I want to.'

'But what about weekends?' Joel persisted, determined to extract as much information as possible from Carleton's father, the man he'd been told was one of the world's great batsmen. He was beginning to believe that his informant had just been having a joke.

Mr Birkby shrugged. 'Sure, when I'm at home. But again, my business takes me away for longish spells that can last over weekends.'

Then, unexpectedly, he laughed quite uproariously. 'Still, reckon I make up for it when I do get a game! Isn't that so, Carley?'

Carleton nodded. 'Guess it is, Dad. You hit everything in sight – out of sight! That's what you always say.'

That was Edward's chance and he seized it. 'Oh, you're a batsman, then, are you, Mr Birkby?'

The West Indian's eyebrows shot skywards. 'Well, of course, Edward, *of course*. What else would anybody want to be?'

'Er, well, some players might, er, like to be a bowler – a fast bowler,' Edward said cautiously.

'Great heavens! Great rainbows in the sky!' Mr Birkby was intoxicated by that idea. 'Bowlers, man, are only there for one thing – to be *slaughtered*. To provide food for a hungry batsman to feed on. No other purpose. Isn't that so, Carley?'

Edward, thoroughly discomforted by that attitude, turned to see what Carleton's reaction would be. Carleton's face was expressionless, however.

'That's what you always say, Dad,' was his neutral response.

'You're a bowler yourself, then, are you?' Mr Birkby asked Edward with some hint of sympathy in his voice.

Edward nodded, a trifle glumly. 'But I bat a bit as well,' he added. 'In fact, I could be classed as an all-rounder.'

He gave Joel a steely glance, defying him to deny that claim. Joel, who shared much of Mr Birkby's view, just grinned.

'Tell you what, then,' Mr Birkby said brightly, looking from one boy to the other, 'you can come and have a coaching session at our place. I'll have a look at your techniques and see if there's any room for improvement. You've been good enough to support Carleton today, so I'll support you in your cricket. What do you say?'

Joel was taken aback by the offer. Like Edward, he wasn't at all sure that Mr Birkby really was a brilliant batsman – or even any kind of batsman, come to that. So what sort of coaching could be expected at his place, as he put it?

'Well, that's very kind of you, Mr Birkby,' Joel said cautiously. He'd been trying to catch Carleton's eye but without success. He suspected that Carleton didn't really approve of the invitation. 'Er, when do you have in mind for us to be there?'

'No time like the present, or so everyone tells me, so let's make it tomorrow,' was the brisk answer to that. 'Come in the morning and then you can have some lunch with us. You know the address, do you?'

In unison, Joel and Edward shook their heads.

'Well, it's easy to find, man. Our place is called
60

The Anchorage and it's down Sancton Lane – you know, by the river. Can't miss it. And, anyway, everyone around there knows Ralph Robertson Birkby. See you guys about ten o'clock, O.K.?'

In unison, they nodded.

Six

As he swung his cycle off the main road by an old
stone bridge and turned sharply into Sancton Lane
the following morning Joel was still wondering
whether the trip would prove to be a great waste of
time. He and Edward had discussed the visit at
length and decided they ought to turn up because
they'd more or less promised they would. Joel was
as keen as ever to discover all he could about
Carleton's background but he seriously doubted
whether Mr Birkby *was* an outstanding cricketer
and a capable coach from whom he could learn
something.

Edward had been the more reluctant of the two
to turn up. Much as he fancied the idea of improving his batting skills, he didn't care for the thought
that Mr Birkby might simply use him as the bowler
for everyone else to practise on in the net (if there
was a proper net). Carleton's father had been so
scathing about bowlers in general that Edward had
begun to dislike him. After all, as Edward had

pointed out to Joel, batsmen *needed* bowlers just as much as bowlers had to have batsmen to bowl at – otherwise there would be no game of cricket. So it was really stupid to go around hating a number of your fellow cricketers simply because their talents were different from your own. Joel, he was pleased to learn, totally agreed with that view.

'Wouldn't mind living around here myself, you know,' Joel observed as they free-wheeled down the incline towards the river. 'Very peaceful, isn't it?'

'Bit too quiet for me,' Edward responded. 'I like things to be happening all around me – more excitement that way. That's why I'm an all-rounder, I suppose. Means I'm always in the game – bowling, fielding close up, *batting*. You know.'

Joel grinned at that artless piece of self-advertising. 'Yeah, I get the point, Ed. Well, if Ralph Robertson Birkby is as good as that chap said he was, you're bound to learn something that'll help *your* batting. Needs it, too, doesn't it!'

They had to resume pedalling as the lane flattened out and entered a wooded area. The houses were located behind high wooden fences or avenues of trees and, in most cases, couldn't be seen at all from the lane.

'Must be about here somewhere,' Joel muttered. 'Funny name to give a house, though: The Anchorage. Sounds as if it ought to be in the middle of the docks or something.'

'Probably got a colossal lawn that runs down to the river where Mr Birkby ties up his yacht,' Edward surmised. 'We'll probably have lunch on board, sunbathing on the deck and sipping iced ginger beer.'

Before Joel could comment on that vivid picture a figure suddenly darted out into the middle of the lane from behind the shelter of a large tree.

'Hey, Carleton, good to see you,' Joel exclaimed. 'We were just wondering – '

'Listen, Joel man, you've got to do something for me,' Carleton interrupted him agitatedly. He seized Joel's hand on the handle-bar as if to emphasise the importance of what he was about to say. 'You must not say anything to my dad about my batting against Empleby. Don't tell him I got any runs or anything. He thinks I just helped out with the fielding because that's all I told him. So you tell him no different, man. O.K.?'

Joel, naturally, was bewildered. 'But *why*, Carleton? I mean, you were terrific in that match – wish I'd batted half as well. Your dad's obviously very keen on cricket so – '

'Man, you don't know the pressures I'm under! So, please, Joel, don't make things worse for me. I didn't ask my dad to invite you for coaching but now I've got to go along with it. Look, I'll make a deal with you, O.K.? You don't tell too much and I'll go on playing for your team – help you win the Knock-Out Cup. That's what you want most, right?'

'Well, yes, but it's going to be difficult – keeping quiet, I mean, if your dad asks me direct questions.' He paused. 'Still, I don't want to let you down – and if you'll play a *full* part in every single Cup match . . .'

Edward, straddling his machine as he patiently listened, decided it was his turn to extract a promise. 'I think you owe us an explanation of some things, though, Carleton. Tell you what: I won't say anything to your dad, either, as long as you tell us about his background as a cricketer – all the main details. You see, we've been told he was a great batsman, good as the best Test player for the West Indies, but we've no proof at all. Oh yes – and you've got to explain why you *hate* batting when you're so good at it. That's a fair arrangement, isn't it? I swear I'll keep my side of it.'

While Carleton deliberated how to answer that Joel looked at Edward with a new respect. It occurred to him that perhaps after all Ed had the makings of a good vice-captain of Shipstone Juniors.

'Look, I just can't tell you all that now, man,' Carleton said, frowning hard. 'There's just no time. My dad's waiting for you to turn up and get started on the cricket. I had to sneak out when he had a phone call from one of his partners.'

'All right,' Edward conceded, 'but you've got to tell us everything before we go home.'

Carleton shrugged and then nodded, resignedly. 'But, come on now. Otherwise Dad'll be searching for me.'

He led the way through the next gateway into a wide drive, flanked on one side by dense shrubbery and on the other by an avenue of trees beyond which there appeared to be an unlimited expanse of smooth lawn. At the end of the drive stood the house; built of mellow brick with twin columns supporting a balcony at first-floor level. Its white paint glistening in the strong sunlight, it was un-deniably a handsome property.

'Hey, you really *do* have a yacht!' exclaimed Joel

as he caught sight of a boat tied up at a landing stage reached by a gravel path from the sloping garden. 'Ed thought you might have.'

'No, it's not a yacht, man,' Carleton replied, managing a grin. 'Just a little motor cruiser. Dad's always been nuts on boats – that's why he went into the shipping business in the first place, I guess.'

'Hello there!' Mr Birkby, strolling into view round the corner of the house, greeted his visitors. Immaculately attired in white flannels, he was already wearing batting pads as if impatient to begin an innings. 'Glad you could make it.'

Rather formally, he shook hands with them and then inquired whether they'd like any refreshments. 'No? Well, we'll have a drinks interval when you need a break! Right, then, let's go and get started and see how you shape up.'

He led his by now bemused visitors through a small orchard at the back of the house to a cleared area where a couple of nets had been set up in a completely professional style. Awaiting them, and calmly tossing a cricket ball from hand to hand or spinning it fiercely with snapping fingers, was another man wearing an orange-coloured cap with a large peak, but otherwise dressed for the game and Mr Birkby introduced him as Ben Murray, adding, 'He's one of my best mates, is Ben. Likes cricket and boats almost as much as I do.'

Ben Murray stroked his upper lip through his blond moustache and then laughed. 'I'm not one of

67

his best mates when I flatten his stumps!'

Mr Birkby watched carefully as Joel delved into the cricket bag he'd brought with him and then garbed himself in pads and gloves. He picked up his bat and aimed a few extravagant strokes.

'Lay your bat down on the ground, Joel – face down,' Mr Birkby unexpectedly instructed him. 'Go on. Right. Now pick it up again.'

Looking as amazed as he felt, Shipstone's skipper did as he was told. He could only assume that Mr Birkby was about to indulge in a practical joke or organise some bizarre training game.

'Ah, now that's where you can improve right from the start,' Mr Birkby said, taking the bat from him and demonstrating a different grip. 'You had your hands too far apart, man. When you grip like that you don't get the power into your strokes that you do when your hands are closer together. You see, you can always tell how a player is going to grip from the way he picks his bat up from the ground. You know the correct way, Joel?'

Joel blinked and then admitted he'd never thought about it.

'Well, it's O.K. to do a lot of things by instinct, Joel. But this time your instinct is wrong. You should pick the bat up as if you were going to chop down a tree! Yeah, as if it were an axe!'

After allowing Joel to play a few air shots to accustom himself to the new grip Ralph Birkby asked his friend Ben to send down a few deliveries.

Edward, already fascinated by what was going on, was thankful that he wasn't expected to do all the bowling. He knew now that he was going to enjoy the day and probably pick up some useful tips on improving his batting.

Joel dealt nervously with the first few balls he received, especially as Mr Birkby was quick to interrupt to suggest improvements in his stance and method of striking the ball.

'The first essential is to get your foot in line,' he insisted more than once.

Eventually, however, Joel settled down and began to enjoy his batting again. Mr Murray rang the changes in his bowling, mixing out-swingers and yorkers with leg-cutters and the occasional perfectly straight ball. Several times Joel's wicket was knocked askew but Mr Birkby told him not to worry about that. The main thing was to feel comfortable at the wicket and to pick out the ball to hit – or, as the coach expressed it, 'give the full treatment to!'

Edward shared the fielding duties with Carleton and was delighted when he received high praise from Mr Birkby for hanging on to a catch at ankle-height. As usual, Carleton made everything look easy.

'Are you going to have a go at batting?' Edward asked him quietly at one point.

'Not if I can help it!' was the immediate response.

Soon it was Edward's turn to go into the net – and he, too, promptly discovered that his batting

70

technique was not yet perfect. His back swing, he was told, was a shade too high; but as it *was* only a shade he was pleased to think that recently he'd sensed that flaw himself and very nearly corrected it. Now he was advised to follow through with his shot when he made one; but his action in over-confidently padding a ball away drew a sharp reprimand.

'You've got a bat to hit the ball with, man! Don't try and use a pad for that purpose. If an umpire's got any doubt at all in his mind, he'll give you out leg-before-wicket wherever the wicket was at the time! Padding up is the shortest route to trouble.'

'Sorry,' Edward muttered, and meant it.

After that, however, he came in for a lot of praise – and he couldn't help reflecting that his batting seemed to have impressed Mr Birkby rather more than Joel's performance. Still, there was one difference he supposed he had to take into account: Mr Murray hadn't bowled so fiercely at him as he had at Joel. On the other hand, Joel was an opening bat ...

'O.K., then, I think it's my turn now,' declared Ralph Birkby happily, seizing his own bat and striding towards the stumps. 'Let's have a look at your bowling action, Edward – see if it matches up to your batting.'

Edward descended from his cloud with the speed of a returning space satellite. The idea of bowling at someone who'd been described as one of the world's great batsmen was terrifying. Even his most brilliant in-swinger would probably be hammered out of sight.

In fact, Mr. Birkby played his first couple of deliveries with some caution, as if to give Edward confidence. Soon, however, he was cutting and driving with power and freedom. It wasn't difficult to see, Edward decided, that Carleton's father was an experienced and elegant batsman, quick to get into position even for Edward's most wayward deliveries (and there were certainly a few of them).

'Right, Edward, I think you've earned a rest,' the batsman called after he'd bowled the equivalent of three overs. 'Your turn, Carleton, then we'll all have a break.'

The Shipstone players looked on with astonishment as Carleton meekly accepted the ball and swung his arm over a few times as if to loosen the muscles. After all, he'd never said he could bowl or shown any interest in trying his hand. Now, as he drifted in to try his luck with his father, he gave the impression that he'd never sent a ball down in his life. Mr Birkby treated the mixture of lobs and half-volleys and even something approaching a beamer, with contempt. The ball hurtled back past bowler and fielders like a bullet. Joel managed to parry one drive and was left wringing his fingers for several minutes.

Then, without warning, Carleton suddenly changed his approach. His saunter became a fast clip: the ball he bowled drew his father forward, beat him completely by pace and turn, and demolished the off-stump. Ralph Birkby turned to survey his wicket, thoughtfully replaced the stump in its proper position and then, with a half-grin, remarked:

'Bit of a freak, that one, Carley. You'll never be able to do it again!'

Carleton made no reply and his expression didn't change. He simply caught the ball when it was returned, turned and ran in to bowl again. This time the ball positively fizzed off the pitch, eluded the bat as Mr Birkby pushed forward defensively and knocked back the middle stump.

'Hey, fantastic ball, Carleton!' Joel couldn't help exclaiming. 'You can bowl like that for us anytime you like.'

Ben Murray, looking equally impressed by what had happened, inquired, 'Where'd you learn to bowl an off-cutter like that, Carleton?'

Carleton's eyebrows shot up so high they almost merged with his busby of hair. 'Was that an off-cutter, Ben? I'd no idea what it was. Didn't seem anything special to me.'

His innocence appeared so genuine that even Mr Birkby accepted it as such. 'Any bowler can bring off a fluke some time – especially if he doesn't even know how he was holding the ball when he let it go. Just try it once more. I'll believe in miracles if you can do it again.'

Instead, he had a good laugh. For the next ball was so short and innocuous it might have been bowled by a small child. After that, Carleton seemed to lose interest and sent down another poor collection of long hops and full tosses until Mr Birkby called a halt.

He sent Carleton into the house for a tray of refreshments. Rather to Edward's disappointment, they consumed them while reclining on the lawn instead of on the deck of the motor cruiser. Their host asked about the Shipstone team and Joel told him of their successes and ambitions; but, as promised, he made no mention of Carleton's contribution to the side.

After the second spell in the nets, during which Mr Birkby passed on some more useful tips and then batted ferociously against Ben Murray's bowling, they had lunch indoors. Mr Birkby said he had some business matters to attend to at his office in the afternoon and when he left Mr Murray went with him.

'You must come again some time – then we might actually get Carleton interested in being a cricketer,' were Mr Birkby's parting words.

'Come on, then, Carleton, tell all!' Joel demanded the moment the three boys were left on their own.

'Yes, you're not to leave anything out,' Edward added.

Carleton fiddled with the remains of an apple on

his plate as if uncertain how to begin. 'Well, you'll have noticed that Dad really can play a bit, and when he was a schoolboy he was terrific – one of the greatest prospects in the history of the West Indies. That's what my Uncle Eugene – Dad's brother – says, anyway. He played in some representative matches and everybody said he was a certainty for the Test team in spite of being only a teenager. And then his father died, very suddenly. And he owed a lot of money, Grandad did, because something had gone wrong with his import business. But nobody's ever told me just what was wrong.

'Anyway, Dad was the eldest boy so he had to do

something about it. He got the offer of a job in Brazil and that's where he went, into a timber firm. There's lots of valuable timber and valuable minerals in Brazil. Well, Dad started to do pretty well and he paid off the debts. To tell the truth, he made a lot of money – and he likes making lots of money. Well, who doesn't? So he didn't go back to Dominica.'

'But what about his cricket?' Edward asked. 'I mean, did he manage to play in Brazil?'

Carleton shook his head. 'There isn't any cricket in Brazil – well, hardly any. Awful lot of football but he wasn't interested in that. Anyway, after some years he had his own shipping business – lots of exports and things like that. Then he decided to come to England. Two of my uncles are here and Dad found out he could start up a good business here as well. Well, when he got to England he found he liked his cricket as much as ever, except that he was so busy making money he didn't have much time to play for anybody – not regularly anyway.'

'He could have at weekends, though, surely?' Joel suggested.

'Oh, he did, sometimes, up in the Lancashire League. Stood in for some of the top overseas stars when they weren't available for the odd match. Plenty of clubs would have signed him up for a season but Dad said he couldn't commit himself for as long as that. He's a perfectionist – that's what Uncle Eugene says. If he'd accepted a contract for a season he'd have had to do everything absolutely right, turn up on time and so on, because of giving value for money – that's one of his great phrases. So then he decided he'd turn *me* into a great cricketer instead. That was his new ambition. He hadn't managed to make it to the top in cricket but all his talent wouldn't be wasted if I got there. See?'

Joel and Edward nodded, fascinated by the story.

'Of course, he wanted me to be a batsman,' Carleton went on. 'He wanted me to become the Test player he himself hadn't managed to be. So he started making me learn when I was still just a kid. At first, I didn't mind. But then it sort of got on top of me – I dreaded seeing Dad come home because I knew that straight away he'd tell me to get the cricket gear on and go off to the nets. Besides being a perfectionist he's very bossy and he certainly, well, bossed me around. I got so scared I'd make a mistake and lose my wicket that I used to make up every possible excuse to get out of cricket practice. You see, I just knew – felt in my heart – that I'd never be as good as he is. And I didn't want to be second best. Do you guys understand?'

'Is that why you went in for disco dancing, something you could do completely on your own?' Edward asked.

'Dead right!' Carleton admitted, pleased that Edward appreciated his reasoning. 'It's also why I practised throwing and catching – you see, sometimes Dad was held up by phone calls just when he was supposed to be coming out to the nets to teach me how to bat. So I had a lot of hanging around on my own. That's when I started aiming at the stumps from all angles. Also, when Dad himself was batting against Mr Murray and some of his other mates I had to be one of the fielders. In a way, I enjoyed that bit. It was something Dad didn't specialise in. He used to field in the slips with the minimum of effort, as he describes it.'

'But, Carleton, do you *really* still hate batting?' Joel wanted to know. 'I mean, you are pretty good at it, judging by the way you batted for us against Empleby. Without the runs you scored we'd have been out of the Knock-Out Cup in the first round.'

Carleton's hesitation was brief, but it was there. 'Well, I hate it if I know Dad's watching me because I know he'll be finding fault with the way I play various strokes. He's given up trying to turn me into a world-beater but he still treats me as a pupil when he gets the chance. But when I'm on my own, just batting for the fun of it, well, I suppose that's different. No, I don't hate it then.'

He paused and then added, 'In a way, I think I'd quite like to prove that I can succeed at cricket – but in *my own* way.'

'Oh, great!' Joel exclaimed, the relief he felt at that statement evident in his voice. 'I mean, we don't want to lose you, Carleton. With you in the side, we reckon that Shipstone can win a trophy at last – the Knock-Out Cup.'

'Well, there's one thing you'll have to avoid if you want a good performance from me,' Carleton replied. 'You've got to keep my dad away from the ground when we're playing.'

Seven

Almost as soon as Shipstone took the field for their semi-final match against Ventlow Park things started to go wrong for them. Mark Lockett made a valiant but totally unnecessary attempt to catch the ball as it was being tossed around casually from player to player. The ball struck him on the tip of his out-stretched little finger and the bone snapped. Mark, who had to be helped from the field in agony, was out of the match before it started. The umpires, while duly sympathetic, ruled that a team list couldn't be changed after it had been handed to the officials – and they'd been in possession of the Shipstone names for the past half-hour. It would just be bad luck if Lockett couldn't bat but, of course, there'd be no objection to the twelfth man fielding for him.

Then, from the very first ball of the match, a catch went down. Edward Tilden had put everything he possessed into that initial delivery. Ventlow's No. 1 batsman, Potter, was the star of the side and so to remove him early on would be a tremendous fillip for Shipstone. Edward knew the moment the ball left his hand that it was a good one. Potter had to play it – and he did so only tentatively. The ball flew off the outside edge of his bat and straight at the wicketkeeper, Jamie Gillespie.

For Jamie it should have been one of the easier catches of his life, for the ball reached him at chest height. It went into his gloves – and came right out again. His desperate scramble to retrieve it was hopeless.

The chance of removing Potter first ball had gone.

Edward's momentum carried him a long way down the wicket and he slithered to a stop only a few metres from the culprit.

'You idiot, Jamie!' he yelled. 'You'd've held on to that if only you'd get the right sort of gloves. Those have always been too big for you. No wonder you don't catch anything.'

Joel at first slip frowned and then called firmly, 'That'll do, Ed.' He had sensed that the square-leg umpire wouldn't tolerate a slanging match, even one between players of the same side. Privately, he applauded Edward's keenness but he had to maintain discipline for the good of the team.

At the end of the over, during which Potter had got off the mark with a boundary and a couple of singles, Joel had another, quieter, word with his opening bowler.

'You're right about Jamie's gloves, Ed. But why didn't you mention it before so that they could have been changed before the match started?'

'Er, I meant to but I forgot. Sorry.'

The frown became a scowl this time. 'In that case, you're as guilty as he is. If you see something's wrong and you take no action to put it right then you've let the side down. You don't have to be the skipper, you know, to think for the team instead of just for yourself.'

Edward felt like retaliating but instead he forced himself to stay silent. In any case, he knew that the rebuke was justified.

Just as Joel was reflecting that strokes of bad luck usually come in threes the third one occurred. Potter had gone for a quick single and then stumbled slightly when his partner sent him back. Crisp fielding by Barinder Singh resulted in a frenzied appeal by Jamie for a run-out decision.

The square-leg umpire ruled that Potter had made good his ground and therefore was not out. It had to be, in Joel's view, a hairline decision. Somehow, though, it seemed inevitable that it should have gone against Shipstone.

As he stood disconsolately in the slips he reflected that perhaps the fates were catching up with them. It really couldn't be denied that luck had been on their side in earlier rounds of the competition. After defeating Empleby, for instance, they'd even got a bye because the team they'd been drawn against had folded up. They'd had by far the best of the conditions in a rain-affected match in the next round: winning the toss had proved crucial and Joel hadn't hesitated to put the opposition in. Barinder in particular had exploited a soft patch at one end and taken six wickets in five overs. Then, in the quarter final, Joel himself had been given not out when he was fairly certain he'd nicked a catch to the keeper. However, he'd always accepted an umpire's verdict under all circumstances and he did so on this occasion. Oddly enough, although he hadn't been batting at all well before that incident he subsequently blossomed and his 55 was easily the top score in the match.

Even the draw for the semi-finals appeared to have gone in Shipstone's favour. Ventlow Park, it was generally agreed, was easily the weakest of the three opponents they could have faced. So Shipstone was the confident choice of most neutral observers to get to the final. Still, if they couldn't remove Ventlow's best batsmen when the opportunities were there the favourites would quickly become the outsiders, as Joel was aware.

He must, he decided instantaneously, take some positive action to unsettle Potter. In spite of all the tips he'd picked up during coaching sessions with Ben Murray, Edward Tilden was not bowling any better than usual. Indeed, since the disaster of the first ball of the match, it seemed to Joel that Ed had lost both heart and direction. He never liked being taken off but there was no alternative.

'I'm putting Steve Brown on in your place next over,' the captain told his opening bowler. 'We'll save the rest of your overs in case Ventlow try to have a thrash at the end of their innings.'

The change was being made in such a tactful way that Edward felt unable to protest, though he was sure that Joel was blaming him for the team's lack of success to date. He realised he hadn't been bowling at his best but it still was a bit of an insult to be replaced by Brownie, in his opinion.

In addition to his usual seam-up stuff, Steve Brown, a lanky, easy-going boy, could also bowl some useful off-spin – and that was what Joel now ordered. His aim, really, was simply to see what Potter made of it after the conventional pace attack. To his delight, he saw that Steve was able to extract some bounce from the pitch, so much so that when Potter attempted a fierce cut he missed completely. Surreptitiously, Joel moved extra cover round into what was practically a second gully position.

Potter survived that over and the next and it looked as though Ventlow were set for a big score from their openers. However, Steve, flighting the ball better than he'd ever done, induced Potter to try another square cut – and this time the batsman directed the ball straight into Carleton's grasp at second gully.

Joel was overjoyed at the way his strategy had paid such a quick dividend; and Steve, who nor-

mally didn't expect to take the wickets of those at the top of the batting order, was inspired. He had the advantage, though, of Potter's suspicion of what might have happened. On returning to the pavilion, the Ventlow opener had muttered darkly that 'the pitch is doing quite a bit'. Because Potter was such a good batsman, that automatically had sown doubt in the minds of his listeners. They didn't expect to cope very easily with Shipstone's mystery off-spinner. And so, of course, they didn't cope at all. Steve picked up no fewer than four of the first five wickets to fall; and while he was bowling so successfully nobody at all tried to hit him off his length.

The main problem remaining for Joel was how to get rid of the other Ventlow opener, Williams, who was beginning to open out after witnessing so many dismissals at the other end. Joel flirted with the idea of bringing Edward back for a quick burst but decided against it; he had to keep pace in reserve for attacking the tail-enders. Bari had already used up his quota and Andy Ross, the other seamer, was not proving to be very effective. Then, just when Joel was thinking it perhaps would be best to concentrate on Williams' partners, the opener quite unnecessarily got himself out. From one of Andy's poorest deliveries the batsman tried to hit a six over long-on. It was falling just short when Edward, scooting round the boundary at a great rate, pulled off a superb catch at knee-height. Williams looked as astonished as anyone. In Joel's eyes, Edward had thoroughly redeemed himself – and he underlined the point by sprinting fifty metres across the field to congratulate the catcher. Fittingly, that brilliant bit of fielding signalled the beginning of the end of Ventlow's innings.

'Well done, lads,' Joel called out as he clapped his bowlers, led by Steve Brown, off the field. Ventlow Park had totalled 122 from the 27.3 overs they'd batted and Shipstone's skipper believed that target was well within his side's reach. Ventlow's bowlers hadn't anything like the reputation of their batsmen.

Nonetheless, Shipstone didn't make a very satisfactory start. In only the third over Sean Greene hit over the top of a good-length ball and had his middle stump knocked back, a sight that vastly encouraged the bowler, who shortly afterwards had Jason Lupton caught at second slip. At that point Joel had reason to be worried. He, as the other opener, was finding no great menace in the Ventlow attack yet his partners were getting themselves out. What made matters worse was that Shipstone were likely to be a batsman short anyway. Mark Lockett had returned from hospital with his broken finger in a splint and would bat only in an emergency. Joel hoped fervently that it wouldn't come to that but some of his pre-innings confidence had ebbed away.

Tim Elvidge, the Blond Bomber, played a restrained and responsible knock until a rather dubious L.B.W. decision went against him. Barinder Singh was even unluckier, playing on in such a way that the ball no more than nudged the leg bail from its resting place; after that even the perpetual 'Smiler' had nothing to grin about. Joel had persuaded a reluctant Carleton to move up the batting order in the absence of Mark and for a time the Swift–Birkby partnership prospered, as it needed to with half the side gone and more than half the runs to make. In recent matches Carleton had never quite matched his performance with the bat against Empleby, though he'd usually contributed useful runs.

'Don't rush it, we've still got a few overs in hand,' Joel advised him during a midwicket chat. 'But if the ball's there to be hit, well, belt it!'

Carleton followed instructions and got behind a short-pitched delivery beautifully, hooking it for six. He tried to do the same to the next ball, quite justifiably; but, unnoticed by Carleton, a substitute fielder had come on between the deliveries, and by accident rather than intent had stationed himself at deep midwicket. By stepping back a few paces he was able to take a catch comfortably when the ball dropped short of the boundary rope this time. Carleton was furious with himself, Joel was dejected. But the skipper still remembered to send an instruction to the pavilion via the departing Carleton.

'If Steve is out in the next couple of overs, tell Edward Tilden to come in next.'

He might have foreseen what would happen. For

Steve, still rejoicing over his success as a bowler, picked the wrong ball to hit and was quickly dismissed, another L.B.W. victim. Edward, thankful to be promoted, and correctly interpreting it as a reward for his recent improvement in League matches, was determined to survive. He had calculated that his partnership with Joel was the crucial one in the entire innings. In his view, neither Jamie Gillespie nor Andy Ross could be expected to muster many runs.

Joel nodded his approval as Edward, with the straightest of bats, defended dourly for a couple of overs. Satisfied that he had support at last, Joel launched an assault on Ventlow's poorest bowler, a boy trying to bowl off-spin and not getting any turn whatsoever. In one over alone, Joel hit him for three fours and a six.

With Edward contributing the occasional vigorous blow, the pair took Shipstone within sight of victory. The opposition's attack wilted almost completely when Joel struck the returned opening bowler for successive boundaries. Edward, well pleased with one of his own shots, a blistering straight drive for four, stayed until the end so that Shipstone's margin of success turned out to be four wickets.

In spite of the fact that he himself was named Man of the Match for his 70 runs and shrewd captaincy, Joel was far from satisfied.

'That wasn't nearly as easy as it should have been,' he told his team before they could launch their celebrations. 'We only really scraped through today.'

'Oh, come on, skipper, let's enjoy ourselves,' Jamie said lightly. 'I mean, we *have* got to the Cup Final.'

Joel's expression didn't relax. 'That's not enough for me. We've got to *win* the Final. And to do that we've all got to be at our best on the day. So, first, we've got a lot of work to do in training and in the nets. Otherwise, we'll finish up the losers – and nobody remembers the losers in a Cup Final.'

Eight

On Cup Final morning Joel's first thought when he awoke concerned the weather. In two strides he reached the window to yank back the curtains. The view was disappointing: uniformly grey sky and drizzle flecking the glass. Joel wrinkled his nose, glanced at his watch and then remembered some weather lore his mother was fond of quoting: 'Rain before seven, fine before eleven.' Well, it was already after 7 a.m. but from the look of the roofs of the houses opposite it had been raining for some time. So perhaps it would clear by the time he'd had breakfast. He daren't contemplate a postponement of the most vital match of his life.

After doing a regulation number of press-ups and exercises to tone up the muscles in his thighs and legs Joel tugged a comb through his springy fair hair and eyed himself critically in the mirror. He was, he decided eventually, just about as fit as he could be for the supreme test of his leadership and talents. He had done all *he* could to ensure that

Shipstone Juniors became the holders of the Knock-Out Cup.

He stripped off his pyjama trousers and dressed rapidly. Then he picked up the American silver dollar that his Uncle Alex had given him for his birthday the previous week. Dated 1885, it was the oldest coin Joel had ever possessed. More important than that, however, it was, according to Uncle Alex who'd owned it for years, a lucky coin. Joel fingered it wonderingly and then slid it into his pocket. Fervently he hoped it would have its reputation intact after the toss-up to decide who batted first.

By the time he was ready to leave for the County Ground the drizzle had ceased, though there was still no break in the low cloud. Joel was going to walk to the match and he'd chosen his route with care. It was the one he'd followed on his first-ever visit to the headquarters of the county side to see a match they'd won in triumphant style. That exciting introduction to county cricket had fired his own enthusiasm for the game. And now he was to play on the turf that his heroes trod. That in itself was part of the glory of this day.

As he made his way up Jack Hill, the cobbled, tree-lined slope that overlooked the Recreation Ground where he'd played his first five-a-side makeshift match, he thought about the team he was going to lead on to the field. Since the semi-final they'd put in a lot of tough training and Joel had left his players in no doubt about what he expected from them, collectively and individually. He just hoped he hadn't sounded and acted like a dictator. Still, he didn't care too much about being liked. Winning a trophy was more important than that. Now, as he came to the main road that led directly to the County Ground, he made the final decision about the batting order – well, as final as could be until he knew which *team* would bat first. He hoped he was being wise in promoting Carleton to No. 4. The West Indian boy had great talent but somehow he seemed to lack confidence – except, oddly enough, when he was batting in a crisis, as in the first round game against Empleby. With greater responsibility so high in the order Carleton might produce his best form. A similar move had worked well in the case of Sean Greene: he'd batted superbly as an opener in recent League matches.

With Mark Lockett still out of the side they needed a solid start from the top four because his replacement, Johnny Nelson, was more of an all-rounder than a specialist batsman. Edward Tilden had done well since going in higher up, but generally the middle order was not very sound. In Joel's opinion, none of them could really be relied upon to keep an end going in an emergency. Much, he supposed, would depend on his own performance – and the duel, the inevitable duel, with Greenfield's chief strike bowler, Zeke Johnstone. The only player in the Greenfield side of West

Indian parentage, Zeke had taken more wickets than anyone in the Knock-Out Cup competition, and when conditions were in his favour he was a devastating seamer. Joel had already warned his players to treat Johnstone's overs with the greatest caution; if Shipstone could survive against his pace then surely they would be well on the way to winning the Final.

Swinging his cricket bag as nonchalantly as possible, Joel turned into the County Ground through the famous black-and-white gates; and suddenly his heart-beat seemed to quicken. A few of the other players had arrived ahead of him but so far there was an absence of spectators. If the weather improved there'd probably be a reasonable crowd for the match and Joel's parents were among those who'd promised to attend. He hoped that Shipstone won for their sake, too, because he knew he wouldn't be easy to live with if they were defeated.

'Got some armour-plating to protect you, have you?' inquired Ricky Foster, Greenfield's skipper when they met in front of the old-fashioned, rambling pavilion. 'Zeke's been praying for cloud cover to help the swing in the air.'

'Oh, we've got the batsmen who can cope with anything you throw at us,' Joel retaliated confidently.

'Oh yeah, you can count on a few bouncers from Zeke as well!' chortled Ricky.

Joel frowned, recognising that he hadn't come

out best in that exchange. Then his hope of winning the toss was dashed, too. Although he produced the silver dollar with alacrity and sent it spinning high, Ricky called 'Heads!' correctly. It was the call most skippers chose but Joel had put his faith in the words on the other side of the coin: 'In God We Trust'.

Ricky, of course, was delighted and, just as predictably, asked Shipstone to bat. Zeke Johnstone was already rubbing his palms together in gleeful anticipation of such a rich haul of wickets that he'd be the only contender for the Man of the Match award.

Sean was wincing as he buckled on his pads in the pavilion. Tim Elvidge, who had always fancied the idea of being an opener himself, asked him what was wrong.

'Got a bit of a stomach ache,' Sean admitted. 'Just sort of came on when I arrived here.'

'Scared, are you? Of E-z-e-k-i-el Johnstone?' It was part of Tim's philosophy to reduce Zeke's threat by expanding the bowler's name to its full length.

'No, of course not. He can be hit – like any other bowler,' was the defiant answer. All the same, Sean was definitely looking paler than usual, as Barinder Singh remarked with a typical wide smile. Bari had dropped down the order to No. 7 and was unlikely to face Zeke at his fastest unless it was during the last couple of overs of the innings.

As the batsmen left the pavilion to a chorus of 'Good lucks' from team-mates, Zeke was tossing the ball impatiently from hand to hand and casting approving glances at the cloud cover. No more than of average height, he was stockily built with the true paceman's well-muscled shoulders. Joel had faced him in league matches without too many qualms. The Shipstone skipper felt that he himself was in good form and that was what mattered on the day. He was relaxed enough to enjoy surveying the County Ground from an unique standpoint: the middle of the square. It was a moment to savour, for he'd dreamed of such an opportunity for years.

By now a small crowd was occupying the best seats in the Members' Enclosure and there were scatterings of spectators beside the sight-screen and along the midwicket boundaries. Joel made no attempt to catch sight of his parents. With Zeke preparing to bowl, this was no time for distractions.

Johnstone stormed in and unleashed the first ball of the Knock-Out Cup Final. It rose invitingly outside the off-stump and Joel cut it for two very satisfying runs; and breathed a sigh of relief as he completed them. Nothing bolstered confidence like scoring off the first ball of the day. The next ducked in to the batsman but Joel's angled bat instantly killed its intentions. Just as he'd expected, the bouncer was the fifth ball. His timing, though, was faultless, as he whirled and swept his shot behind square leg for the initial boundary of the innings. The applause from Shipstone supporters was gratifying and Joel waggled his bat in acknowledgement. Predictably, Zeke looked furious as he completed his unsuccessful over.

Sean Greene was thoroughly relieved, of course, that he'd not had to face Zeke at the start of his innings. Greenfield's other opening bowler, Smart, was nowhere near so troublesome; Smart's main weapon was his nagging accuracy once he'd found a length. So Sean, following instructions, played himself in carefully and contentedly and he managed to avoid an encounter with Zeke in the latter's second over, too. But, in its way, that absence of contact contributed to his undoing.

It was in his third over, following some words of advice from his captain, that Zeke got everything right. Instead of striving for still more speed or greater bounce, he switched his aim to the stumps – and made a proper allowance for the swing of the ball in the heavy atmosphere. His reward was immediate. Sean tentatively stabbed at the first Johnstone delivery he'd received – and lost his middle stump. In his exultation Zeke jumped almost as high as one of his own bouncers and then whooped down the wicket with his arms waving above his head.

Shipstone's first wicket had fallen with their score on 26 – and the second fell at the same total. Jason Lupton, the left-hander who'd been having a poor season, never saw the ball that got him plumb L.B.W. Joel, who'd been thinking earlier of dropping Jason from the side, wished now he'd done so. His main concern, however, was with Carleton, the next batsman. Would he be good enough to keep Zeke at bay when the bowler had suddenly discovered his touch?

Carleton looked calm enough as he took guard. But he didn't waste any time in getting to the other end after averting the hat-trick by pushing the ball away on the off; his acceleration was almost matched by Joel's, for the skipper had anticipated Carleton's reaction.

Joel dealt capably with the next ball and then comfortably took a single off the last ball of the over. He was still thinking about the team's position as Smart came in to bowl a new over – and the airy shot that Joel played was his worst of the season. Simply because he wasn't facing up to the dynamic Zeke he didn't concentrate properly; and the penalty was being caught behind the wicket off a thin edge. The entire Greenfield side celebrated the departure of the opposition's captain and leading batsman.

He was so angry with himself that he didn't say a word to Tim Elvidge, the incoming batsman, or respond to the sympathetic cheers in the Members' Enclosure. It would be a long time before he'd forgive himself for such crass carelessness: even though he was out for 13 he couldn't for a split-second put that down to bad luck.

There wasn't much anyone in the dressing-room could say to him for it was plain the skipper was furious at losing his wicket. Joel, dismayed by the gloom caused by the collapse of three wickets for just two runs, decided as soon as he'd removed his pads to take a walk on his own round the ground. It might help him to think clearly how to lift his team and get them back into the match with a hope of winning it.

He was deep in those thoughts as he turned the corner of the pavilion and practically bumped into a familiar figure.

'Hi, Joel, I was sorry to see you out like that,' Ralph Robertson Birkby greeted him. 'But, really you know, you'd no business fishing for a ball like that way outside your off-stump. Why, if – '

'Oh, Mr Birkby! I don't want to be rude but I wish you weren't here,' gulped Joel. 'I mean, Carleton says he can't bat at all if he knows you're watching. And in a white suit like that, well, you're a bit, er, conspicuous, so he'd be bound to see you soon. We really *need* his runs, too, as you can tell from the scoreboard.'

Ralph Birkby was understandably taken aback by such a welcome from his son's friend. But he was smiling his acceptance of the situation when the attention of both of them was seized by a drama on the field. Tim Elvidge was down on his haunches, holding his head, after being hit by a steeply rearing delivery from Zeke. Other players were beginning to cluster around him and an umpire was signalling for medical aid.

'I'd better go and see how bad it is,' exclaimed Joel, beginning to move away.

'You do, man, but just listen: if the boy's got to go to hospital I can get him there faster than anyone in my car. And that'd remove me from the scene for Carley's benefit, wouldn't it?'

In fact, hospital treatment was just what Tim did need to repair a gash on his temple. Tim was making light of the injury but that was in his nature because he was fearless both as batsman or suicidal fielder. Joel assisted him from the field as play was resumed and delivered him into the hands of Mr Birkby.

'Let's hope Carley hits you out of trouble,' his father remarked as he started the engine of a luxurious saloon.

Joel nodded sombrely. 'If he doesn't, I think we've lost this match.'

Nine

As he watched Johnny Nelson trying desperately to
fend away some of Zeke's fiercest deliveries, Joel
wished that he'd sent in either Bari or Edward
ahead of the newcomer. Clearly the exuberant Zeke
had been given another over at this stage in the
hope that he could add to the destruction; and Joel
couldn't see Johnny surviving much longer the way
he was playing.

He was right. In the same over Zeke claimed his
third official victim with another indisputable
L.B.W. appeal against the hapless Nelson. So, with
only 38 runs on the board, Shipstone had lost half
their wickets – for it seemed beyond a possibility
that Tim would return to make any further contribution to the match.

Head down, Joel trudged back to the pavilion –
and his return to the dressing-room was only sixty
seconds ahead of Carleton's. With the departure
from the attack of Johnstone and Smart, Carleton
had decided to launch an all-out assault on the

second-line bowlers, a spinner and a moderate medium-pacer. But he'd miscalculated the degree of turn on the spinner's best ball and been stumped easily. He'd made 16, and thus was the side's top scorer, but he was thoroughly dejected at getting out in such fashion.

'You've usually batted so well when we've had a crisis – like the Empleby match,' said Joel, uncertain whether to be sympathetic or angry.

'Yes, but nothing was expected of me then, was it? I mean, today was a bit like it used to be with Dad – I was *expected* to be terrific. That's why you put me at No. 4.'

'Your dad was here today, Carleton,' Joel admitted. 'But I sent him away so you wouldn't spot him and go to pieces. Actually, he was very helpful – he rushed Tim to hospital to get urgent treatment. So it was a good thing your dad came.'

Carleton looked mortified. 'Sorry I've let the team down, Joel. But I'll make up for it in their innings, I swear.'

For a time, Bari and Edward resisted well and were starting to push the score along, when Edward was over-ambitious about a second run to a shot that went down towards third man; the return was low and fast and Edward was run out. Jamie and Andy didn't last much longer, but Bari, farming the bowling cleverly, kept Shipstone's faint hopes alive in the partnership with Steve Brown.

The score crept above 70, but that was still less

than half the total Joel had hoped for before play began.

Then Shipstone received an unforeseen boost to morale: the return from hospital of Tim Elvidge, his wound impressively bandaged. Joel leapt to his feet at the sight of him, suggesting he should immediately lie down and rest. Tim, however, declared that he felt fine now – and that he had every intention of resuming his innings. Hardly were the words uttered than Steve's gallant rearguard action came to an end with short extra cover taking a simple catch. Even before Steve had taken half-a-dozen strides towards the pavilion, Tim was buckling on his pads and reaching for his bat. Foiled in his efforts to persuade Tim not to go in, Joel could only wish him luck and agree with him that Shipstone really did need every run they could get.

The unlikely appearance of the bandaged hero rather unnerved the Greenfield bowlers and Tim, always willing to have a go at almost anything, made the most of some poor stuff in the remainder of the over. A ferocious pull for four and a drive of great power were vintage Elvidge.

The end, however, was not long delayed, though it came at the other end when Barinder, as if trying to emulate his new partner, unwisely swung at the third ball of Zeke's last over; and Gully took the catch, two-handed, above his head. So Shipstone had been dismissed for 81, with Barinder Singh joint top scorer on 16 and Tim Elvidge not out 6.

'It could, I suppose, have been worse,' remarked Joel to his team after congratulating the last wicket pair on their valuable contributions to the total. 'But it's going to take a super-human effort by the bowlers to get us back into this game with any chance at all. Fortunately, the cloud hasn't lifted so there should still be some swing in the air for us, too. And remember, everybody – and I do mean *everybody* – fielding is going to be vital. We can't afford to give 'em a single run because of slack fielding. We've got to save everything, every single one of us.'

Although Tim was keen to field, and claimed that he was perfectly fit, the umpires ruled that he would be taking an unwarranted risk, and so the twelfth man replaced him. When the Shipstone players filed through the Members' Enclosure on to the field Joel noted that Mr Birkby was now sitting on the front row. He was glad to see, as he turned, that Carleton and his father exchanged greetings.

He was soon in action. Greenfield's left-handed opener, anxious to get off the mark, punched Barinder's third ball into the covers and scampered down the wicket. Carleton collected the ball so fast that the movement was no more than a blur. In his own eagerness to do well, his throw was a little wild: and, because Jamie didn't take the ball cleanly, that made all the difference. By the finest margin the batsman regained his ground in time. All the same, the quickness of the fielder alarmed the entire batting side.

Progress was slow. Though not getting any extravagant movement through the air, Bari and Edward pinned the batsmen down with sustained accuracy. The fielding generally was enthusiastic and sharp. Joel was delighted with the way his players were responding to the challenge. But one problem remained: wickets were not falling. Overs were ebbing away from Greenfield, who were scoring at a rate that was painful to their supporters. On the other hand, they had all wickets in hand for a violent assault on Shipstone's second-line bowlers.

'Bari, I'm taking you off after this over unless you get a wicket – I've no real option,' Joel confided. 'So give every ball everything. O.K.?'

Smiler smiled his understanding and did as he was asked. And, to his own great joy, he made the first break-through. A well-pitched-up ball forced the left-hander back on his stumps – and, with the merest touch of his heel, he dislodged the leg bail. It was Jamie's screech of excitement that told the batsman he was out.

Greenfield's first wicket had gone down in the eighth over when they had only 17 runs on the board. Even so, they still needed just 65 to win at less than three an over. However, the new batsman took a long time to settle in and then, never having looked comfortable, he gave a stab at a faster ball from Andy Ross and diverted it into his stumps. Thoroughly elated, Andy produced a much better ball for the next batsman who missed it completely and was L.B.W. Suddenly, the game had tilted in Shipstone's favour.

Ricky Foster strode to the wicket in a manner that proclaimed he was going to play a true captain's innings and win the match off his own bat. Steve Brown was the bowler he chose to smite – and Steve suffered cruelly as fielders were forced back and the scorers worked over-time. Quite rapidly, the odds swung back towards Greenfield. The perspiring Steve strove to recover his line *and* bowl faster: and then, when Foster smashed the ball back at him, the bowler made a desperate effort to cling on to it. But the blow was too fierce, the ball ricocheted away and Steve's right hand was split. The pain was so severe the bowler almost fainted before spectators came forward to take him into the pavilion and provide medical aid.

Joel's face was now nearly as pale as the victim's. Another bad injury was more than his team could bear. The match was surely slipping out of Shipstone's hands. For Steve was supposed to bowl another three overs and there was really no one in the side to replace him.

'I'll take over from Steve if you like, Joel,' Carleton said quietly as the players moved to new positions between overs. 'I've had plenty of practice at bowling, remember.'

'Oh yes, sure!' Joel agreed, recalling Carleton's success in the nets against his father. He ought to have thought of that idea himself. Could Carleton's bowling be Shipstone's salvation?

It hardly looked like it when Foster contemptuously swatted away Carleton's first delivery and at the same time brought up the 50 for Greenfield. The next ball was no better and Foster pulled it into the crowd. Joel gritted his teeth, Carleton frowned and adjusted his grip across the seam. The next ball, on an ideal length, zipped in from the off and laid Foster's leg stump flat. Greenfield's captain gazed at the wreckage in total disbelief. His chief ambition for some time had been to hit the winning run.

Carleton, having shaken off the acclaim from his team-mates, very nearly penetrated the guard of the next batsman next ball. Then, with the final ball of the over, he had the newcomer sweetly taken in the slips by Joel. Now, half the Greenfield side was out; but only 25 runs were required for victory.

Zeke Johnstone, sent in early because of his ability as a hitter, erratic though it was, quickly got the chance to show that his eye was in – and the sufferer was Andy Ross. A six into the Members' Enclosure was actually fielded by Mr Birkby.

Zeke's downfall was caused by taking an extra run at the end of the over. Now he faced his fellow West Indian. Carleton tempted him, Zeke hooked and, down at long leg, Edward Tilden made up for his disappointment at not so far taking a wicket by taking an electrifying catch. Wrathfully was how

Zeke departed. His mind had been mainly on the Man of the Match award.

Panic, not surprisingly, set in among the Greenfield batsmen; the next one in was so determined to avoid further contact with Carleton that he was run out by more than half the length of the pitch from the second ball he received. With the last ball of the over Carleton induced another feeble stroke so that the catch at forward short leg was the easiest of the match.

After Andy had snapped up his first wicket in the next over the game seemed to be over. But the last wicket pair resisted so well that the Greenfield total began to creep up again; what's more, luck was going their way. Snicks and edges failed to carry to fielders, yorkers were dug out miraculously, wild swings sent the ball soaring over the heads of the slips. Joel knew he had to keep Carleton on but who should replace Andy, his stint now completed? He decided on Barinder. Smiler smiled like a rainbow and calculated that *he* would be the one to win the match by clean bowling the defiant last man.

Another inside edge that unbelievably missed the stumps provided the No. 11 batsman with a further run – and, suddenly, the margin between the sides was down to six. One tremendous heave by a batter could win the match for Greenfield. The boy facing Carleton saw it as a hero's shot; the entire fielding side simply saw the possibility and hearts were palpitating with frustration and fear.

Carleton switched his grip on the seam again and zig-zagged in to bowl. It was far from being the best ball he'd sent down. The batsman saw it well, then closed his eyes, swung with all the force he could summon up – and made contact.

From the meat of the bat the ball rocketed away. Anyone with eyesight good enough to follow its course would have sworn it was going for a straight six. But Carleton, leaping high to his right, flung up a hand. The ball struck the palm, shot upwards in an almost vertical climb – and then, as it fell, Carleton, twisting sinuously, grasped it with both hands as he himself crashed down on to the turf. It was at least the equal of any of his athletic feats while disco dancing.

'The catch of a lifetime – fantastic!' yelled Joel as he hauled Carleton to his feet. 'You've won the Knock-Out Cup for us. Fantastic!'

'Well, you picked me for my fielding in the first place,' Carleton managed to say before Shipstone's supporters, who now included his father, could seize him and chair him from the field in absolute triumph. 'And any player always fields best to his own bowling. Right, man?'